"You're much too serious," he said

"And you're despicable," Laurel ground out with loathing.

"Despicable," he repeated, and that seemed to amuse him, too. "How very English you are. Now if I were English we could talk about something safe—like the beastly weather we're having. But I'm not English and I'm never very safe. Is that what frightens you about me?"

"I'm not frightened of you," Laurel lied. "I'm just not interested."

"Yes you are." He reached for her hand and kissed the wrist he'd bruised. "I'm sorry if I hurt you, but I can't guarantee I won't do it again unless you stop running away from me. There's something between us that we'll have to do something about sooner or later. So stop teasing and make it sooner."

Anne Beaumont started out as a Jill-of-all-writing-trades, but she says it was her experience as a magazine fiction editor, buying stories and condensing them for serialization, that taught her to separate the bones of a story from the flesh. In her own writing she starts with her characters—"a heroine I can identify with, then a hero who seems right for her." She says that many writers work in reverse—plot first, then characters. "That's fine," she says. "If we all had the same method, we might all be writing the same books, and what a crashing bore that would be!" In addition to Anne Beaumont's contemporary romance novels, the author has written historicals under the pen name of Rosina Pyatt. She lives on the Isle of Wight, with its sparkling white beaches, and has three children of whom she is immensely proud.

Another Time, Another Love

Anne Beaumont

Harlequin Books

TORONTO • NEW YORK • LONDON
AMSTERDAM • PARIS • SYDNEY • HAMBURG
STOCKHOLM • ATHENS • TOKYO • MILAN

Original hardcover edition published in 1989
by Mills & Boon Limited

ISBN 0-373-03049-5

Harlequin Romance first edition May 1990

CHAPTER ONE

JUST after midnight the phone rang for the umpteenth time. Laurel Curtis propped the receiver on her shoulder. 'Newsdesk,' she said, carrying on tapping out an update on a royal security scare story, her eyes and mind on the VDU screen.

'Got you first time. That was a lucky guess! I thought I might have to ring around a few papers to track you down,' said the breathy, lively voice of her best friend and ex-flatmate Shirley Dixon.

'Shirley, what are you doing up with the night owls?' Laurel asked, her fingers still moving over the keyboard, determined to get the last sentence of her story finished. 'I thought all good magazine writers were tucked up in bed by now.'

'Yes, well, some of us like to be naughty and live a little sometimes. You should try it, and there's no time like the present. I'm over at Tony's and, guess what, he and Janine have just got engaged, the mad, impetuous fools! We're having an impromptu party—all the old gang, or near enough. Come and join us.'

Laurel had been reading over her story while Shirley spoke. It would do. She pressed the button that would send it to the sub-editors' desk and sat back and relaxed. She yawned, stretched and replied, 'Not me, Shirley. I'm for bed when my shift finishes. Give my love to Tony and Janine, and tell them I'll catch up on the congrats another time.'

'Don't be such a pain,' Shirley scolded. 'There's more to life than working, you know. What happened to the old to-bed-with-the-larks-and-to-hell-with-tomorrow girl I used to know?'

'She grew up, and it's already tomorrow. Sorry, Shirley, but another time . . .'

'That's what you're always saying. Come over, just for half an hour, otherwise we're bringing the party over to your place.'

Laurel hesitated and looked at her watch. Less than an hour and she was off shift, and she knew Shirley was capable of carrying out her word. 'All right, but just half an hour,' she conceded. 'You know what a flap and panic a freelance's life is. Things have piled up and I've a busy day tomorrow—today.'

'See you,' Shirley said, 'and don't forget, if you don't show up we'll all be on your doorstep.'

Laurel went to the party, intending only to show her face, but it was so good to be among old friends that for once her rigid self-discipline broke down. She was still there at six when somebody started cooking breakfast.

She didn't get home to bed until seven, forgot to set the alarm, and woke up at three in the afternoon with the better part of the day gone. She was angry with herself, and a bit bothered. Was she tiring, seventeen months too soon, of the spartan way she ran her life?

Well, whatever, she was running late and her next shift started in three hours.

Laurel splashed cold water on her face, zipped into

a buttercup-yellow track-suit, programmed the overloaded washing machine and was sitting down drinking tea as it groaned and lurched its way into the beginning of its cycle.

She scanned the headlines of the stack of news-papers she had delivered every day, left them to read more thoroughly later, and carried her cup over to her telephone answering machine.

There was only one message. It was from Dyson Enterprises (UK) Ltd to say representatives would be calling on her that afternoon to make an offer for the lease of her flat and, this time, would she please be there?

Laurel looked at her watch and pulled a face. She didn't have time for property developers right now. Dyson Enterprises (UK) Ltd weren't the only people in a hurry. Food and sleep were things she grabbed when and where she could, but she couldn't keep up the pace of her life unless she stayed fit, and that meant regular exercise.

A few minutes later she was slamming the front door of her top-storey flat and heading for the stairs. The other three front doors up here in the gods were already boarded up to keep out squatters. Very depressing.

Sighing, Laurel pushed her thick, fair hair under a bobble-hat, missing a few strands that waved errati-cally about her face, then she was off down the stairs. She passed more boarded-up flats on every landing, but here and there a few were still inhabited, making her feel less like the last survivor of the Alamo.

On the last flight, Laurel checked her pace. A group

of sober-suited city types, each man carrying an important-looking clipboard, were milling around the grimy, narrow, Edwardian entrance hall, blocking her way to the dilapidated double front doors.

Damn, the property developers she didn't have time for. Laurel jogged lightly on the last step to signal her impatience to be on her way, and said pointedly, 'If you please, gentlemen . . .'

Laurel didn't realise what an incongruous splash of colour, beauty and vitality she made on that dingy staircase and, instead of standing back, they gaped at her. Impasse, then both front doors were pushed open and a tall, bronzed, loose-limbed man breezed into the hall.

He was casually but expensively dressed in fawn trousers, roll-neck fawn sweater and a suede jacket, as different from the city types as it was possible to be but, for all that, his effect on the clipboard men was magical.

They surged towards him like satellite planets that had just found their sun, murmuring respectfully, 'Mr Dyson, sir.'

Laurel smiled in cynical amusement at their fawning attitudes. Connor Dyson himself, no less. The boss. What was he doing slumming here? She thought property tycoons clinched the deal, then left their minions to tidy up the details. Funny she should be one of those 'details'—a tenant who'd been too busy to take a cheque and go.

Then her smile faded. Connor Dyson looked at her. From her vantage point on the bottom stair Laurel's china-blue eyes met Dyson's steel-grey, and her precise and highly organised world rocked.

It was a timeless look of recognition, of deep awareness. They were total strangers, and yet they stared at each other with the intimacy of lovers.

Once before Laurel had experienced a similar look, and to discover she was susceptible to another frightened the life out of her. She wasn't a green and gullible girl any more, but there was no mistaking the sensations flooding over her, the sudden rush of excitement, the leaping pulses, the thumping heart, the glowing warmth.

And she was done with all that.

Once scorched, and her flesh had taken on the resilience of asbestos, or so she'd thought. Laurel searched his face for something that would jar on her, repel the magnetism. She searched in vain. The more she saw, the more she melted.

Vaguely she was conscious that the photographs she'd seen of him in the gossip columns hadn't done him justice. No photograph could, because Connor Dyson wasn't a strictly handsome man. His face had a rugged toughness, the kind that improved with hard living, and the power of his attraction came from a force within.

His cropped, light brown hair waved crisply, the ends bleached white by the sun, and his eyes reflected his inner power. They were that arresting shade of grey that had the X-ray effect of looking into and through everything. As he was looking into and through her now.

Laurel found she was quivering with anticipation and fought for control. A sensual, predatory male, she told herself, hoping a cynical revulsion would set in, but all the time her heart kept thumping out the response his eyes demanded of her.

Anger at her unexpected vulnerability turned Laurel's gaze into a glare. She saw his eyebrows draw together in a frown, and that broke the spell. She was able, several seconds too late, to look away from him.

She saw a gap in the businessmen, threaded her way through it, and was slipping past Connor Dyson at the door when he said, 'Hang on a minute—are you Laurel Curtis?'

His voice was pleasant, unhurried, unmistakably Australian. The sound of the Great Outback to go with the look of the Great Outdoors. Laurel liked it so much, she reacted with uncharacteristic rudeness. 'Yes,' she replied, 'and goodbye.'

'Wait.' Connor Dyson stopped her the only way he could, by grabbing her arm. 'I'm Connor Dyson——'

Laurel brushed his hand away, horrified at the tingling messages his touch transmitted to every nerve in her body. 'What am I supposed to do, curtsy?' she interrupted, then she was through the door and running down the shallow steps to the chilly sanity of the street.

She had to look back. The power of his stare forced her to. Their eyes met again, with the same devastating effect, and then she was running on, her colour heightened. She was ashamed of her rudeness, even more ashamed that a chance encounter could arouse the slumbering menace of her own sexuality. And after all this time.

She couldn't believe it. She didn't believe in love. Alan had cured her of all that, and the cure had held good for four years.

There had been no more leaps in the dark for her. No more falling flat on her face. No more picking herself up, piecing together the splintered fragments of a trusting heart and weeping over the bits that were missing.

She was a different woman now, with different ambitions, heavy responsibilities. True, the pattern of existence she'd mapped out for herself was a bit warped, but it was workable—and safe.

Mockingly, an image of Connor Dyson rose before her eyes and she felt most unsafe.

Laurel ran on, lecturing herself, getting herself together. The past four years had taught her to attack problems before they attacked her, and Dyson was just another problem. Remove his interest in her, and she'd remove the man—and his interest was in her flat.

Soaring property prices in London had thrust this shabby district upmarket, and Dyson was one of the speculators buying cheap to renovate and sell high. He'd bought Hewitt House and its three sister blocks, and now tenants like Laurel, who had endured the neighbourhood in its rough days for its cheap rent, were being bribed into selling their leases.

OK, she thought, she'd find the time to negotiate, and be done with the man.

By this time Laurel had run all the unwanted sensations Dyson had aroused out of her system. She headed back. The hall of Hewitt House was quiet, empty. She walked up the stairs, her eyes bright, a dew of perspiration covering the roses in her cheeks, straying tendrils of hair clinging damply to her lovely face. She'd lost her city pallor and was looking like the country girl she really was.

It was late October and cold enough for her breath to steam the air as she climbed the stairs. On the second-storey landing she saw Dyson again, about to enter a flat with his clipboard men. Her treacherous pulses leaped with excitement once more, and she thought even if he'd been dressed the same as his companions he would still have looked different. Not so decently civilised, which was another way of saying not quite so tame.

Mentally tough, emotionally shot to pieces, by the time she was level with him on the landing her eyes once more blazed with that defensive hostility that was so peculiarly her own, and once more he frowned.

'Miss Curtis,' he began politely, reaching out to stop her.

Laurel shied away. 'I'm sorry, I can't talk now. I'm much too rushed.' She hurried on. It was only several flights later, when she reached her flat, that she realised he must think she was being deliberately awkward to get a bigger pay-off than anybody else.

That hurt because it wasn't true, it was only a result of being stupid enough to play eye-games with a sun-tanned Casanova. She worked on newspapers, she knew how often he was in the gossip columns with one socialite after another on his arm. The only thing she could say in his favour was that he was an honest womaniser. Alan had been devious . . .

Shrugging the pair of them to the back of her mind, she entered her immaculate flat, so different from the decay and neglect outside her front door. She stripped and padded barefoot into the tiny bathroom, climbing into the bath to get under the shower and swishing the plastic curtains closed so she didn't soak the floor.

The shower was one of Laurel's own improvements, along with the storage heaters that kept the damp at bay up here under the ancient roof. Apart from that the flat was nothing more than a base, a jumping-off spot for the home and more regular way of life she was working so hard for.

Her goal was in sight. Another seventeen months and she'd have the satisfaction of knowing that, without a scrap of help from Alan, she'd coped. That was motivation enough to keep to the straight and narrow, even if a disturbing man *had* thrust himself into her life.

'Damn,' Laurel said. Connor Dyson had slipped into her mind again. She dried herself with unnecessary vigour, slipped her feet into comfortable mules and went into her kitchen-cum-living-room wrapped in a soft towelling robe.

She pulled the clothes out of the washing machine, slapped them in the dryer and went over to the telephone. She dialled the Mayfair number of Dyson Enterprises (UK) Ltd, spoke to the woman who'd left the message and explained, 'I'm too pushed for time to see anybody today. I'll call in at your offices on Monday afternoon at four-thirty.'

'Miss Curtis, you keep making appointments and breaking them,' she was told crossly.

'I work funny hours, but I'll be there without fail on

Monday. I don't enjoy being hounded.' Laurel put the phone down. Immediately it rang again. It was Paul Collyer, the sports editor of the paper she worked most regularly for.

'Laurel, love, can you play rugby?' he asked.

Freelance reporters got used to being asked weird things, but this was something new. 'I know some of the dirty songs,' she answered flippantly, and so she did. She'd done her stint of cheering on the sidelines on freezing, winter weekends. Alan had played rugby until his handsome nose had almost been broken, frightening him off for life.

Why, today, did everything keep coming back to Alan? She blamed Connor Dyson for making waves in what had been calm waters.

'Good enough,' Paul came back. 'We're sponsoring you for the Ladies of the Press versus the Celebrities charity match, the second Sunday in November.'

'What's wrong with your staff girls?'

'We decided you'd look best in shorts, love. It's all in a good cause, to raise money for a kiddies' hospital. I'll fill you in with the details later. Cheers!'

The line went dead. Laurel grimaced, switched on the microwave and shoved in a meal picked at random from the freezer. While she was eating it, she caught up on the papers. She was flicking through the popular tabloid she was working on that night when there he was again. Connor Dyson, smiling out of the gossip page at her.

The man was haunting her.

Laurel turned the page savagely. A few seconds later she was turning back, unable to resist reading the paragraphs accompanying the photograph.

From them she learned that Aussie property tycoon Connor Dyson, thirty-five, and Lady Letitia Hinds, twenty-two, were a regular twosome at London's more exclusive nightclubs. After that, the copy became coy, speculating whether the Earl's daughter would marry Dyson when her divorce from Aussie racing driver Carlton Hinds was finalised. The lady, it seemed, had a thing about Australians. There was also a hint that Dyson had bought Cherisham Manor in Hampshire from Lady Letitia's father with marriage in mind. The manor was one of the Earl's lesser estates, but there was nothing wrong with keeping it in the family, so to speak.

The frown between Laurel's eyes deepened. Hampshire! Of all the counties in England, why did Dyson have to pick on the one in which she, too, had a stake? The wretched man really was haunting her.

No, she was over-reacting. Her village was a good ten miles from Cherisham, and the chances of meeting down there were remote enough to be non-existent. Unless Dyson did intend marriage, and his track record said differently, he wouldn't have any intention of living there. Buying the estate was probably just another bit of property speculation.

Still, she felt unsettled and irritable as she tidied away her meal, folded the washing on top of the dryer to be ironed tomorrow, and got herself ready for work.

There was also a slight hint of panic about her as she quickly teamed a yellow jumper with a charcoal-grey suit and low-heeled shoes. She didn't want to meet Dyson again and she was trying to work out how long it would take him to get up here to the top floor. Long enough, hopefully, for her to be well away.

Laurel gave her hair a quick brush, grateful that its thickness and natural wave saved it from needing much fussing, and grabbed a fur-lined raincoat from her wardrobe. There was no guarantee she would spend the shift in the newsroom, and she had to be prepared for anything.

Once she'd gone in for a night's work and ended up spending three days in Amsterdam on a drugs bust story; another time she'd ended up in Spain covering a plane crash, to say nothing of almost a week in Scotland chasing runaway teenage lovers. It was all grist to the mill and money in the bank, which was what her life was all about at the moment.

Laurel had a hasty look at her face. Her clear blue eyes and healthy complexion needed no extra colour, but she put her make-up case in her handbag, clipped her radio-pager to her skirt belt and had a last look round.

The flat was pin-neat, far too neat for anybody to live here. Well, she didn't really live here, she existed—and survived. It was all she asked for.

A characteristic glance at her watch and Laurel hurried out of the flat. She ran lightly down the stairs, her raincoat over her arm, her handbag banging against her side and her fair hair bouncing on her shoulders. Then she saw that her timing was appalling. Dyson and his entourage were just on the way up.

She speeded up, neatly skimming past Dyson, with

a breathless, 'Sorry, still can't stop. I've fixed a date for your office, Monday afternoon.'

Laurel raced on down the stairs, taking with her a memory of Dyson's frown and the look of frustration in his eyes. Her nerves jumped. He didn't look the sort of man who took kindly to frustration. What was the big rush, anyway? According to the letters she'd been bombarded with from his company, he didn't want everybody out until April. Another six months.

Hewitt House, built in the time of horse-drawn carriages, boasted no garages. Laurel's economic little red runabout was parked outside in the street, and it was all but hemmed in by a fabulously expensive silver sports car. It had to be Dyson's. Nobody in this back street owned a status symbol like that.

She had to do some tricky manoeuvring to get her car out, but that seemed the last of the day's aggravations. The traffic flowed as smoothly as she could expect at this time of night, and she was in the newsroom with time in hand.

Laurel, who would have welcomed the diversion of being out and about, was kept in the office that night, rewriting stories other reporters phoned in and making the routine hourly calls to the Press offices of the police, fire and ambulance services. Around eight-thirty the first edition came up, and just after that her radio-pager bleeped.

The phone number that flashed up when she pressed the button was Shirley's. She dialled it, saying, 'Still awake?' Shirley couldn't have had any sleep at all last night.

'Am I ever,' Shirley breathed. 'I tried to get you

earlier, but you'd already left for work. I'm still in the office, it's been one of those days.'

'Hard luck,' Laurel replied, meaning it. She and Shirley went back a long way. They had met at college, doing a journalism course, trained on the same London local paper, shared a flat and knew just about all there was to know about each other.

When Laurel had joined a freelance agency to get daily newspaper experience, Shirley had switched to magazines. Laurel had met Alan, their paths had parted, and it was Laurel who had gone nowhere while Shirley had risen rapidly to become features editor of a glossy weekly. She'd put a lot of work Laurel's way at a time when it had been desperately needed.

'It's not so much hard luck as no luck at all,' Shirley replied. 'I'm in a flap. One of our features has fallen through and we're rushing through a substitute—a survey ten years on of famous women who married toyboys.'

'What's new about that?' Laurel asked.

'Who can be fussy when the devil drives?' Shirley came back. 'But these marriages have lasted. Our slant is whether it's love or common sense that keeps these marriages together.'

'Love or common sense? You're talking about opposing factors,' Laurel objected, and for some reason she had a mental image of a bronzed face and steel-grey eyes. The niggle at the back of her brain that was Connor Dyson was with her again.

'Well, you can't beat opposing factors for a bit of spice, and that's what we need for the fifth interview.

The others are fine, but this one's a dud. A reporter-photographer did it for me, but she's obviously more used to working for the knit-yourself-a-royal-family type of magazine. Her stuff's too bland, it needs your bite. Could you do a new interview in double-quick time? The deadline's Monday.'

'Shirley, I'm sorry. This is the last weekend in the month, the one I always spend at home, and tomorrow is Friday. I'm taking off at noon for Hampshire.'

'I know, that's what makes you so perfect. The new interview is set for tomorrow afternoon. The subject is the feminist author Dolly Camden and she lives just outside Petersfield, which is on your way. She's fifty and still married to a playboy-type yachtsman fifteen years her junior. If anybody can find out how they paper over the cracks in their relationship, you can. Please,' Shirley urged, 'don't say no. If you set out an hour earlier, you can still arrive home on time. I just need some good quotes. Phone them over and I'll weave them into the stuff we already have.'

'I wouldn't do it for anybody else . . .' Laurel grumbled.

'Bless you! Brian Hobart is taking the new pictures. Can you give him a lift down? His driving ban still has a month to run. He'll get a train back. Shall I tell him to be at your place by eleven?'

'A minute later and I won't stop for him. I hate anything disrupting my long weekend home,' Laurel warned.

'He'll be there, and he'll have a copy of the dud story to put you in the picture about Dolly. Thanks a million, Laurel. That's one I owe you.'

Laurel hung up, and after that she was caught up in one of the flap and panics inevitable on a newspaper putting out four editions a night, but when that crisis was sorted out another one started. It was just one of those nights. She was due to finish at one a.m. but ended up doing two hours' overtime.

It was a very weary Laurel who filled out her worksheet and gave it to the news editor to sign. She felt drained and, with her resistance low, Connor Dyson slipped back into her mind. She tried to chase him out. He wouldn't go.

Laurel drove home grim-faced through the silent streets, trying not to feel as though a pair of grey eyes were watching her, or that the brain behind them knew what she was thinking and feeling.

She tumbled into bed, only to be tormented by images of him in full glorious Technicolor. Laurel groaned and pulled the quilt over her head. Only when she drifted into sleep and her thoughts drifted into dreams, over which she had no control, did her face soften and her lips smile.

It was a happy time and it ended all too soon.

Laurel wasn't sure what was waking her, and resisted, persuading herself hazily that it was only the mail being delivered. The sound came again, no mere rattle of the letter-box or ringing of the bell, more of an outright assault on the knocker.

She felt as though she'd only been asleep five minutes. Her heavy eyelids refused to open and she staggered out of bed, groped for her dressing-gown, threw it over her shoulders and trailed like a sleepwalker to the front door.

She fumbled with the lock and opened it, expecting the postman with a package too bulky to go through the letter-box. She forced her eyes open and saw Connor Dyson. Spruce, bronzed, exuding health and vitality. Laurel leaned wearily against the doorjamb, her eyes losing the struggle to stay open. She must still be dreaming.

Her fair hair was tumbled, her dark lashes cast darker shadows on her sleep-rosed cheeks and her dressing-gown slipped from her shoulders to the floor. She didn't know she'd lost it, and drooped there innocently in a voluminous winter night-gown that revealed nothing except bare toes.

The dream that was Dyson didn't say anything and she forced her eyes open again. She saw him staring at her toes and stared at them as well. That was when she saw her dressing-gown on the floor. She reached for it at the same time he did, felt her hair brush across his cheek and then their hands touched.

The dream seemed to be continuing, because it seemed to Laurel that they stayed like that for ages until dazedly she straightened up. So did Dyson. She saw he had the gown, held out her hand for it, but then she was in his arms and his lips were on hers, as though searching for an answer to a question they were both asking.

Laurel was too surprised to resist, and it was only when he released her that the world came back into focus, outrage flooded through her and she raised her hand to slap him.

He was expecting it and caught her wrist. 'Just to

teach you not to answer the door like that again,' he said angrily, and she wondered wildly why *he* should be angry. Then he was adding, as if she hadn't got the message, 'You're an open invitation to rape. Don't be such a stupid little fool again.'

Laurel wasn't little and she wasn't normally a fool, but he was right enough to make her surly, more on the defensive than ever. She took the gown he thrust at her, slipped it on and fumbled with the belt. 'I forgot to put on the safety chain. I'm usually careful, but I didn't know you were going to come crashing on the door in the middle of the night,' she retorted because, to her, it *was* the middle of the night.

'It's eight o'clock in the morning,' Dyson snapped, then, apparently exasperated at her belt fumbling, he pushed her hands away and tied it for her.

Laurel went rigid, stepped back and exclaimed, 'Keep your hands to yourself! And if it's only eight, you can go back to wherever you came from.'

He seemed to make a great effort to collect himself, and said more pleasantly, 'I'm sorry I shouted. You'll have to stop making me mad. Why don't I make coffee while you dress, then we can talk about your lease?'

'At this hour?' Laurel pushed him back as he took a pace towards her. 'Are we all supposed to be on Australian time or something? I'll negotiate the sale of my lease in your office on Monday afternoon, as I've already told you.'

'Yes, you're great at making appointments, better still at breaking them. Keep it up and you'll be the only one left in a deserted block. You'll be begging me to get you out. Our terms are generous enough without this cat-and-mouse game, so do yourself a favour and be reasonable.'

They were glaring at each other and Laurel ground out fiercely, 'You'll get nowhere harassing me at this time of day. Where the devil do you get your nerve from?'

'The same place you get yours. Since you're never available at a reasonable time, I had no choice but to catch you before you left for work,' Dyson snapped back.

'Left? I've only just got home!' It wasn't strictly true, but Laurel was in no mood for exactitude.

'A likely story. What kind of work do you do?'

'I'm a stripper,' she snarled, and slammed the door.

CHAPTER TWO

WHATEVER Connor Dyson thought, she might have guessed he wouldn't just give up and go away. He hammered on the door and shouted, 'I'll be back at noon. Be here.' Only then did it go quiet.

Laurel stalked back to bed. At noon he could knock down the door if he wanted to. She wouldn't be around to listen. It would do him good to learn he couldn't push some people around without getting a shove or two back.

She felt a certain savage satisfaction about that, but mixed in with it was a twinge of unease. Deep down she knew this whole silly situation really had nothing to do with the lease any longer. He wanted to buy and she wanted to sell, if the price was right. She didn't want to be left alone, as he'd pointed out, in a boarded-up building.

No, it had become personal. She'd started it by being unreasonable and objectionable because she was frightened of the powerful way he attracted her, but now he was being just as bad. It was tit for tat, kids' stuff. That was laughable, not frightening.

And yet her unease persisted into her sleep and her dreams were troubled . . .

Promptly at eleven Brian Hobart was on her doorstep, attractive face pale, brown hair tousled and hazel eyes ringed with weariness. His camera straps were looped over sagging shoulders and his casual clothes looked as though they had been slept in.

'Rough night?' Laurel asked with a great deal of fellow feeling.

Brian yawned. 'I was at Heathrow until seven this morning to picture for posterity the return home of some ghastly pop group or other. They were due in at three, but the flight was delayed and delayed. You know how it is. By the time I got home it wasn't worth going to bed so I flaked out in an armchair. How was your night?'

'So-so.' Laurel didn't want to think about it. She'd only got up half an hour ago. She and her weekend-bag were ready, but she'd had no time for breakfast and the ironing wasn't done. It irritated her, falling below her efficiency standard.

She picked up the zippered holdall in the hall and suggested, 'Shall we swap hard luck stories in the car? This is supposed to be my weekend off.'

Brian, like Shirley, was a friend from the old, carefree days. He took her bag and shambled down the stairs beside her, scolding, 'You know, Laurel, you shouldn't confuse a chap when he's at his lowest ebb by wearing tight trousers and kinky boots.'

'Happily married men shouldn't get confused,' she retorted, knowing he adored his wife and two little sons.

'That's it, nag me, it might make me forget your kinky boots. How's everything? Long time no see and all that. Sorted out Mr Right yet?'

'What's there to sort?' she replied flippantly. 'All the best men are married.'

'Flattery, darling,' Brian said, putting a friendly arm around her shoulders and giving her a squeeze, 'will keep me awake where all the nagging in the world will fail. Ask Daphne, she'll tell you.'

They both laughed, and that was how Connor saw them when they came out of Hewitt House. He was across and a bit further down the road, reversing into a tight parking space. He knew he was obstructing the traffic, but he paused to study Laurel.

She was a riveting figure in knee-length boots, fitted blue trousers and a chunky-knit blue sweater. The cold October sunshine gleamed on her fair hair, and Connor remembered how cuddly she'd looked when it had been all tumbled and dishevelled when she'd answered the door to him earlier.

He also remembered her bare toes and how protective he'd felt. Needlessly, he thought, his mouth hardening, as he looked at the man with her. The fellow was scruffy, but his arm was around her as though he were exercising exclusive territorial rights. He was the one who should have got out of bed to answer the door.

Connor felt a curious sense of loss. He didn't have time to analyse the feeling, because he saw the scruffy fellow throw a weekend-bag into the back of a little red car and climb in the passenger seat while Laurel walked round and opened the driver's door.

They looked as though they were sliding off for the weekend and he had an appointment with her at noon. He was only half parked, but he had started to get out when an irate hooting from the car behind, which he was obstructing, forced him to change his mind.

The hooting made Laurel turn her head. She looked down the street and her eyes met Connor's before he jumped back in to finish parking. Laurel jumped into her car and was zooming away by the time he got back out of his.

Brian waited until Laurel straightened the car after careering round a corner and observed plaintively, 'There's a difference between keeping me awake and frightening me to death. I was banned for less.'

'Sorry.' Laurel eased up on the accelerator. She was stupid to let Connor Dyson panic her into driving like a maniac. She hadn't confirmed the appointment and, besides, he was an hour early. To catch her out? Well, he was the one who had been caught, and she had nothing to feel guilty about.

Yet she did feel guilty, and more uneasy than ever. She bit her lip as the thought came unbidden that it wasn't Connor she was running away from, but herself. An impossible task, even for her, and she mustn't start thinking of him as *Connor*. That made him more of a threat, somehow.

'Did we have the hounds of hell on our tail or something?' Brian asked mildly.

Laurel ducked the question by asking, 'Haven't you got some background stuff to read over to me?'

'Will later do? I've got half a ton of lead on my eyelids. I'd like to get a snooze in first.'

'You could have stretched out in the back . . .'

'Don't worry about me. I can sleep anywhere, any time,' Brian mumbled, and promptly proved it by snuggling down in his seat and going out like a light.

Laurel drove through the busy London traffic and

was able to put her foot down when she picked up the
A3 to the coast. She forgot about Brian beside her. If
she had any companion in her car, it seemed to be
Connor. She just couldn't get him out of her mind.
She was becoming obsessed, and there was no space in
her life for an obsession. Particularly with a man like
him.

Yet she felt in some indefinable way he was already
a part of her. He provoked, stimulated and infuriated
her, not by anything he did or didn't do, but by just
existing. It wasn't his fault. She shouldn't hate him
for that. But she did.

Her thoughts and feelings were so tangled, so
hopelessly in opposition, that fifty miles passed like
five, and with a start she realised they were almost
there. She woke Brian and, when he'd read over the
previous interview, he commented, 'Dolly Camden
sounds like a tough old bird. Always up to her neck in
demos, and churning out one feminist book after
another.'

Laurel, at twenty-six, was a long way from middle
age, but she demurred, 'Fifty's not old these days.'

'It must be like a hundred when you've got a toyboy
husband.'

'I'll ask her about that.'

'Are you kidding? She'll eat us for lunch. I'm glad
I'm only along to take the pictures.'

'Jammy beggar,' Laurel mocked.

But Dolly, when they met her, although formidable,
was also fun—and she loved being provocative. Laurel
had no trouble getting her quotes, and she was
mystified as to why the previous interview had gone

badly until Dolly explained, 'You've read my stuff, so you know what I'm all about. The last girl just glanced through a few books and thought she could bluff me. Ha! I made her work hard for nothing to teach her to do her spadework next time. I always do mine before I write a line.'

'Which,' Brian commented as they drove away, the interview nicely buttoned up, 'made me wonder what time you'd had to get the jolly old spade out.'

'Just luck,' Laurel replied. 'I read most of her books at college.'

She dropped him off at the railway station in Petersfield and carried on heading south. She stayed off the motorway, preferring the slower, peaceful country lanes, the fallen leaves of autumn crunching under the tyres, her soul seeking a renewal of purpose and spirit.

This was a world away from Hewitt House, and when she reached her own village she felt she'd shed her city image and was restored to something of the girl she'd once been. As she turned into the driveway of the quaint old house, roofed in the manner which gave it its name, The Pantiles, her eyes were on the downstairs window. The face she was expecting to see was there watching for her.

She reached in the back for her bag and got out of the car. By the time she'd straightened up the front door was open and a small figure was flying towards her.

'Mummy!'

Laurel dropped the bag and caught Lianne as she hurtled into her arms, burying her face in the soft, fair hair so like her own. She was home. Safe. Now she could expect the threat that was Connor Dyson to be licked into perspective—and banished.

Laurel looked from her daughter's scrubbed bedtime face to the next drawing on the pile. She'd successfully identified the forest of purple sticks as grass, and now she had to figure out what the overgrown red centipede in the middle of it was. Tactfully she observed, 'Very colourful. Tell me about it.'

Lianne leaned forward from the pillows, stabbed at the centipede with a chubby finger, then pointed at the dog curled up on the rug beside the bed. 'It's Shadow!'

The dog stirred at the sound of her name and thumped her bushy tail. She raised her black and white collie head, weighed down by what looked like spaniel ears, and stared hopefully at her little mistress.

No illicit invitation to jump on the bed followed, and Shadow, two years old and too well-trained to break the rules without an express command, dropped her head back on her paws.

'Of course it's Shadow,' Laurel agreed. She saw her daughter yawn and kissed her cheek. 'The Sandman's knocking at your door, darling, and he won't go away until you're fast asleep. Time to give Shadow her hug.'

'Can she come up on the bed? Just for a tiny minute?'

Laurel glanced at the door. She hadn't heard Uncle John come home, so Aunt Sue would still be busy in the kitchen. 'All right, just a tiny minute.'

In fact it was five minutes, while Laurel put away the drawings and tidied up the toys. Uncle John had built shelves into the recesses on either side of the boarded-up fireplace to hold the soft toys Laurel brought home for Lianne, and still they overflowed on to the cupboards and floors.

Finally Aunt Sue had called a halt, telling Laurel severely, 'You're over-compensating Lianne because you can't be with her all the time. It isn't necessary. She knows she's loved. All you're doing is spoiling her. She'll still expect gifts when you're living here permanently, and she won't understand why she doesn't get them. Put your money in the bank where it will do both of you more good.'

Aunt Sue had been right, as usual. Now Laurel fetched down only those small things a mother would normally buy her child from week to week: chalk, crayons, simple jigsaws.

Laurel found it hard, though, to resist the teddy bears and other cuddly animals she fell in love with herself and knew Lianne would adore. Perhaps it was herself she'd really been trying to compensate for missing so much of Lianne's baby years.

With herself and the child to support, and the future to be provided for within a limited time, what choice had she had? If Alan had been a different sort of man . . .

Laurel tried to check her thoughts, but they ran on, probing the old wound to see if it was still festering beneath the surface.

Of course it was still festering! Her whole attitude

was proof of that. Betrayal, it seemed, was so much harder to get over than love itself. If only she could think of Alan with some kind of softness, a bitter-sweet regret, she might begin to heal. Yet she couldn't. He'd made her despise him and there was no coming to terms with that.

She only wanted to strike back, and her targets were the men who'd tried to take his place. Feeling nothing, it had been easy to stay remote until Connor Dyson came along. He was different. He got through to her. He——

'Night-night, Shadow,' Lianne murmured to the dog.

Her voice brought Laurel back to reality. She found she was twisting a teddy bear in her hands, her knuckles white, and she forced herself to relax. She shooed the dog off the bed and gave her daughter a hug, breathing in the clean smell of freshly brushed teeth and the sweetness of baby talc. 'See you in the morning,' she said.

'And the morning after that?' Lianne asked.

'Yes, and one more—Saturday morning, Sunday morning and Monday morning.'

'Goody. When will you be rich enough to stay for always?'

Laurel stifled a sigh. Always the same question, and the answer didn't vary much. 'Seventeen months, around the time you start proper school.'

'I'll be a big girl then,' Lianne said, and Laurel smiled down at the small face so like her own, with the same fair colouring and blue eyes. Alan's eyes had been brown and his hair dark. She couldn't see a trace of him in his daughter, but it was wrong to search for this characteristic or that. Lianne was her own person and she mustn't try to make her otherwise.

Laurel couldn't understand why she was even thinking of Alan. She didn't normally. It was as though Connor Dyson, by threatening her future in some vague way, had unlocked the door to the past.

'Tomorrow,' she promised, straightening up, 'we'll put on our wellingtons and jump in puddles if it rains. If it doesn't, we'll rake up all the leaves and have a bonfire at the bottom of the garden.'

'Goody,' Lianne breathed again, but her eyes were closing. Laurel clicked her fingers for Shadow to follow and crept out of the room, leaving the door open so the light from the passage would shine through.

Downstairs, Aunt Sue was setting the table in the dining-room. She was almost as tall as Laurel, slender and quietly elegant in a tweed skirt and green twinset. She was over sixty, but looked a great deal younger. She'd been a beauty once, like her younger sister, Laurel's mother. But unlike her younger sister she had no use for charm or vanity and was often blunt to the point of rudeness.

She had a kind heart tempered by a shrewd, practical streak that kept her from being soft, and she didn't like help with the chores, claiming that it only hindered her. Laurel got on well with her, not least because she knew when to stay out of her way.

'Is the little madam settled?' Aunt Sue asked, deftly slotting the napkins into their holders.

'She's not that bad, is she?' Laurel asked, dismayed.

'She would be, given half a chance.'

Laurel relaxed and laughed. 'Wouldn't we all?'

Shadow shot to the door and began leaping up with whines of excitement. 'Uncle John's home,' Laurel interpreted. 'Perhaps I can make myself useful now by pouring the sherry.' They were an old-fashioned couple, and even though she was grown up now she'd never been invited to call them John and Sue. It amused her but, like Shadow, she was too well-trained to break the rules.

Uncle John came in, going straight to the fire and rubbing his hands against the chilly damp of the autumn evening outside. He was smaller and plumper than his wife and Laurel didn't think, bless him, that he'd been allowed to make a decision since his marriage thirty-five years ago.

Laurel kissed his cheek, gave him his sherry and was predictably scolded, 'You look as if you're still working yourself to skin and bone.'

Just as predictably she replied, 'Nonsense, I was never fitter. I love my work, you know I do.' Not, she thought wryly, that she had much choice.

The weekend was now safely launched on its usual course, and always before she'd welcomed the sameness after her hectic life-style in town, but as they sat down for dinner she felt something was missing. She wasn't content and she should be. Everything she wanted was here.

Surely Connor Dyson's disruptive influence hadn't penetrated this far? With the chilling coldness of icy fingers on her spine, she realised that it had. After four years of single-minded effort, it wasn't enough to be Laurel Curtis, mother, and Laurel Curtis, reporter. She wanted to be Laurel Curtis, woman, with all that that entailed.

That was enough of a jolt, but Aunt Sue had another for her. When they were on the dessert, she said, 'Uncle John is taking voluntary redundancy, Laurel. It means we can retire to Spain in February instead of waiting another eighteen months. Will you still be able to take over the house?'

Laurel looked at Uncle John for confirmation, knowing it was inevitable but dreading it. This would upset all her careful plans. It was like being brought down at the last fence just as the winning-post was in sight.

'Actually it's early retirement with all the usual benefits,' Uncle John explained. 'The bank is being down-graded to a sub-branch, and it won't need a manager any more, just a couple of tellers. If I transferred to another branch I'd have to sell the house anyway, and it doesn't seem worth all the upheaval for such a short time. We've decided we might just as well go straight to Spain.'

'I see.' Laurel sounded calm enough, but her brain was racing. For some years her aunt and uncle had been buying a villa at Torremolinos, renting it out for summer lets to help pay for it when they weren't holidaying there themselves.

They'd always intended to move there permanently when Uncle John retired, and that had given Laurel the idea of buying The Pantiles from them. She loved the old cottage. It was the closest thing to a real home she'd ever known, and it would mean less disruption for Lianne when Uncle John and Aunt Sue moved out of her life and Laurel moved in permanently.

'Will you still be able to afford the house with over a year's less savings?' Aunt Sue asked.

'It will mean a bigger mortgage but, yes, I think I can cope,' Laurel replied slowly, although she didn't really see how she could. Not lightly would she let the house go, though—not after all the effort she'd put in to get it.

'You must bear in mind your income will fall when you work locally,' Uncle John pointed out, 'and old houses eat up money, even when they've been as carefully preserved as this one. I wish we could drop the price but——'

'It's our nest-egg,' Aunt Sue broke in.

'I understand that,' Laurel responded quickly. 'You've helped me enough as it is. I'll have to re-do my sums and let you know. A lot will depend on how much compensation I get for the lease of my flat. I'm seeing Connor on Monday afternoon.'

Drat! How familiar she'd made him sound, trotting out his first name as though it came naturally.

'Connor?' Aunt Sue asked, as Laurel knew she would.

'Connor Dyson, who's bought the flats. He's been round seeing tenants about their leases, chasing up the slow ones, I expect. I was in too much of a hurry to talk to him about mine, so I made an appointment for Monday.'

'But you called him by his first name as though you know him well.'

'In a sense I do,' Laurel replied, as a very lame

excuse occurred to her. 'I'm a reporter and he's always in the gossip columns with some socialite or other. You know, the tycoon-cum-jetsetter-cum-playboy stuff. He's a great womaniser.'

'Oh,' Aunt Sue said dismissively. 'You don't want to get involved with another one of those.'

'I know.' It was what she'd been telling herself since yesterday. Good heavens, was it really only yesterday? Connor Dyson must be some sort of catalyst. Within twenty-four hours of seeing him for the first time, her whole life had been turned upside-down.

First she'd been in danger of losing her well-protected heart to him, and now she was in danger of losing her much-loved house. She didn't know whether she was dreading Monday, or looking forward to it in a way she hadn't looked forward to anything for years.

CHAPTER THREE

LAUREL was still in an undecided frame of mind when Monday came. She delivered Lianne to her playgroup at ten, promised to phone often and to make one of her flying mid-month visits if she found herself with a free day, then set off for London.

She had a lot to do when she got back. There was no time to meander along country roads. She headed straight for the motorway feeling irritated, edgy, and not at all rested.

She knew Connor Dyson was at the core of her discontent. He'd continued to haunt her all through the little treats and pleasures of the weekend like a big bronzed spectre at the feast, if such a thing were possible.

He made her feel her family weekend, the highlight of her month, was never going to be satisfying again unless he were there. 'It's physical,' Laurel announced contemptuously to the windscreen wipers that regularly punctuated her vision. 'Purely physical. I'm not coping too well because I've forgotten what it feels like to be attracted to a man. I've been comatose for too long . . .'

Admitting it, saying it aloud, made her feel tougher. The problem was pin-pointed. Now she'd be able to cope, as always. She might even have felt better if, at that precise moment, a car hadn't roared up beside her in the overtaking lane. It stayed there and she glanced at it.

It was a low, silver sports car with a big, bronzed man at the wheel. For a second Laurel thought the fever in her blood had infected her imagination. She'd been so sure she'd never encounter him down here.

Could it be that fate, having taken a hand in her affairs, hadn't finished with her yet? Don't be so silly, Laurel mocked herself; you'll be believing in fairies at the bottom of the garden next.

No amount of self-mockery, though, could stop the rush of excitement just the sight of him caused her. She tore her eyes from his and stared back at the road. She knew he was still there and felt as though he was willing her to look at him again, but she wouldn't.

Then the silver car zoomed ahead, sticking to the overtaking lane until it was lost in the distance. She felt rejected, as though he'd given up too soon. But she was being silly again. There was no reason why he should want her to look at him. She wasn't anything to him except a thorn in his side. It made her sad to realise that.

Laurel's thoughts were so gloomy, it was a while before she realised the day was darkening like night. There was going to be one heck of a storm. She already had her sidelights switched on because of the drizzle, now she needed her headlights.

When the storm broke it was torrential. It sounded more like metal filings than rain hitting the car, and her windscreen wipers could scarcely keep her line of vision clear. Traffic was reduced to a crawl, and Laurel, seeing the slip-lane to a service station, crawled down it. It would be quicker in the long run to stop until the storm was over than wear herself out trying to carry on.

Other drivers had the same idea, and she followed the lights of the car in front to the parking area. She parked as close to the restaurant as she could, leaped out, locked her car in double-quick time and made a dash for it. She was wearing a thick yellow jumper with her blue trousers and boots, and she only had a short distance to go, but she felt the chill and the fury of the rain before she got under cover.

She shook the rain from her hair and approached the desk where the receptionist allotted tables. The woman was dark-haired, in her forties, and she gave Laurel what seemed an unnecessarily close scrutiny. Then she startled her by asking, 'Miss Curtis?'

'Yes, but——'

'I thought so. "She's wearing a yellow jumper and she's beautiful. Roses in her cheeks, eyes the colour of the sky when the sun's shining and hair the colour of ripened corn." I couldn't miss a description like that, could I? He's waiting for you.' She indicated a table on the far side of the restaurant next to the windows.

Connor Dyson was rising to his feet and going round the table to pull out the seat opposite his. Laurel was stunned. She knew she should snub him and sit somewhere else, but she found herself walking towards him as though compelled to do so. How had he known she would stop here? She hadn't even known herself.

He smiled at her, but she didn't respond. She just sat in the chair he was holding and, when she was settled, she felt his hands on her shoulders. They slid down her arms, slowly, familiarly, and her nerves jumped.

'You're wet,' he said. 'Don't you have a coat?'

'It didn't seem worth the bother. I'll soon dry out.'

'You don't look after yourself very well, do you, Laurel?'

To her relief he'd moved from behind her and was folding himself into the chair opposite. 'I'm very good at looking after myself, thank you,' she replied, and then she saw the little yellow rose in the middle of her place setting. She picked it up. 'What's this for?'

'To say sorry for waking you up on Friday morning.'

Laurel stared into his grey eyes and saw in them an expression that made her feel more out of control than ever. She looked at the little bowl of mixed flowers on the table and then at the bowls on the other tables. Every one had a rose in them except theirs. Now she knew why the rose had such a short stem. 'You've pinched it,' she accused.

'That's all right. I've squared it with the manageress. She thought it was very romantic. So do I. I've never had breakfast with a stripper before.'

Laurel stabbed the rose back into the bowl and snapped, 'I've had breakfast, and I'm not a stripper!'

Connor took the rose out of the bowl, wiped the stem on his handkerchief and gave it back to her. 'I've had breakfast, too, and I know you're not a stripper. You're a reporter and you mostly work nights.'

'How did you find that out?'

'I spoke to George, the caretaker at Hewitt House.' Connor was surprised at the alarm that flashed into her eyes and his tone changed. 'Now what have I said wrong?'

But the waitress came up to take their order. Laurel asked for tea, Connor made it for two, and the waitress took away the untouched cup of coffee that had been in front of him. By that time Laurel had had time to consider. For some reason her defence mechanism, which was always on overdrive when Dyson was anywhere near, warned her not to let him anywhere near her private life. Involvement lay that way, and she was terrified of involvement.

The mere thought of control of her life passing out of her hands into somebody else's brought her out in a cold sweat. She was still, four years on, climbing out of the pit she'd fallen into the last time that had happened, and she'd no intention of being knocked back in.

George, though, was no threat. He'd only worked at Hewitt House for three years. To him she was just a face seen irregularly because of the unsocial hours she worked. She avoided Connor's question by asking, 'How did you know I'd stop here?'

'I hoped. It didn't seem too far-fetched when you consider we have a history of meeting up in funny places. I'm still trying to figure out what a girl like you is doing in Hewitt House.'

'I'm still trying to figure out why you're personally involving yourself in the leases. I'd have thought you made the deals and left somebody else to tie up the details.'

'Generally, yes, but I don't want to talk about leases. That can wait until this afternoon.' He reached across the table and touched her hand. 'I don't think that rose can stand up to much more of that treatment.'

Laurel had been twirling it nervously, unconsciously, between her fingers, but she stopped at his touch and put the rose down. He withdrew his hand but he took his time about it, and she thought she had his measure now. He was expecting her to be difficult this afternoon, and tea, roses and sweet-talk were part of the softening-up process. He must think she was very naïve.

The tea came. Laurel asked, 'Sugar?' and when he shook his head she poured two cups without. She guessed she was supposed to ask what he *did* want to talk about if it wasn't leases, but she wouldn't co-operate. She just sipped her tea and let the silence lengthen. He'd set up this situation—let him fumble his way out of it.

When he did speak, it was abruptly. 'So you didn't go away with that fellow for the weekend, after all?'

Laurel had carefully been avoiding looking at him, but surprise took her eyes to his. 'What fellow?'

'The one who was wrapped around you on Friday morning.'

'Oh, you mean Brian—and he wasn't wrapped around me. We happen to be friends from the old days, that's all.'

'You're not old enough to have any "old days",' he replied dismissively, 'and you were too preoccupied with him to have any time for me.'

It couldn't be jealousy in his voice. He was annoyed because she hadn't put his business with her first. There's arrogance for you, Laurel thought, and was also annoyed.

'You made an appointment, I didn't confirm it,' she pointed out. 'Brian and I had an assignment in Petersfield, which is on my way home.'

'Where is he now?'

'With his wife and children, I imagine. I dropped him at the station when the job was done,' Laurel answered frigidly.

'Where's this home you talk about? I thought Hewitt House was your home.'

'Frankly, Mr Dyson, you want a lot of information in exchange for a cup of tea, and none of it is any of your business!' She gathered her handbag and gloves and moved to stand up.

Connor leaned across the table and grabbed her wrist to stop her leaving. He exerted a lot of pressure to keep her in her seat. When she winced and stopped struggling, he told her savagely, 'I've spent a weekend I'd sooner forget about thinking of you. Everything I thought had a question mark after it. Obviously I need some answers so I can get on with my life, and that means getting to know you. If you don't like it, hard luck. Neither do I, but that doesn't change anything. Just sit there until I can think of something we can talk about that won't cause a riot.'

Her wrist hurt, and his arrogance took her breath away. He seemed to think she was his to command. He let go of her and sat back, but his eyes dared her to move. She didn't risk it. She'd thought at the beginning that he wasn't quite tame, but now he seemed more than half wild.

She rubbed her mangled wrist and said furiously, 'Who opened the cage and let you out?'

The storm passed from his eyes and they gleamed with amusement. 'Love you when you're mad, Laurie,' he said, and smiled.

He was teasing her now, playing with her. Too much money and too many women had gone straight to his ego. She glared her contempt and his amusement increased. 'Somebody has to laugh at you. You're much too serious.'

'You're despicable,' she ground out with loathing.

'Despicable,' he repeated, and that seemed to amuse him, too. 'How very English you are. Now if I were English we could talk about something safe, like what beastly weather we're having. But I'm not English and I'm never very safe. Is that what frightens you about me?'

'I'm not frightened of you,' Laurel lied. 'I'm just not interested.'

'Yes, you are. If you don't like me, it's your own fault. You could bring out the best in me if you wanted, but you don't, so you bring out the worst.' He reached for her hand, pushed back her sleeve and kissed the wrist he'd bruised. 'I'm sorry if I hurt you, but I can't guarantee I won't do the same again unless you stop running away from me. There are more than a few question marks between us, there's something we're going to have to do something about sooner or later. So stop teasing and make it sooner.'

He accused *her* of teasing? He was unbelievable.

Laurel's wrist was burning from the imprint of his lips, and as she snatched it away her cheeks began burning with embarrassment when she saw all the interested faces turned their way, but he obviously didn't give a damn. He was behaving as if she was the only one worth bothering about.

Part of her was thrilled, the other part appalled that she could be falling for what had to be, given his history, a well-practised routine. 'If I had time and space in my life for a man, which I don't,' she retorted scathingly, 'I'd go for one with a bit of finesse.'

'*Touché,*' he replied. 'Not that it will make any difference in the long run. And I'm delighted to hear there isn't another man in your life. That's one of my question marks answered.'

Laurel stood up in disgust, and this time he let her go. She was outside the restaurant and beginning the run for her car when he caught up with her and pulled her back under the cover of the restaurant's awning. 'Your forgot your rose,' he said, tucking it behind her ear, 'and I want you to have it. Believe it or not, it was well meant.'

Laurel refused to look at him, staring rigidly at his shoulder, which happened to be on a level with her eyes. He tipped her face up to his and continued, 'My office, this afternoon at four-thirty. If you don't show up, then I'll know you're afraid of me. I'll be only all the more interested in chasing after you to find out why.'

'Have you quite finished?' Laurel asked bitterly.

'Not quite.' Slowly, deliberately, his lips brushed across hers. It was the lightest, most tantalising of caresses, promising the earth if she cared to follow it up.

Laurel's lips quivered, but she forced herself to stand stone-still and not to react. Oh, he was good, she thought. He was top of the class in the gentle, and sometimes not so gentle, art of seduction. It was all he was interested in, and she, she assumed, was supposed to feel flattered.

Connor looked at her for a long time, then he said softly, 'When you and I first saw each other, something happened. It isn't going to go away, so why are we fighting? We were never meant to, I'll take my oath on that.'

He sounded very Australian, very stubborn and very sure of himself. Laurel was almost mesmerised into believing him, but he would have to be a very different kind of man, and she a very different kind of woman, to permit the trance to go on any longer.

She broke from him and ran to her car. On the way she snatched the rose he'd placed so possessively behind her ear and threw it away. She hoped it told Connor Dyson all the things she hadn't been able to tell him herself.

It seemed her petty gesture had succeeded. No sooner had she nosed her little red car on to the motorway than his silver sports car flashed by, and kept on going. He'd made his move, lost, and now she was dismissed. His ego had taken a battering, and she didn't think he'd want to risk a repeat of the experience. He'd arrange for somebody else to negotiate her lease this afternoon.

Laurel watched the silver sports car until it was out of sight. The end, she thought, of that 'something' that had always been doomed. She'd killed it, just as she'd always meant to. She was safe. She was also very sad, but that would pass.

She drove on, waiting for her nerves and emotions to return to normal, judging normal to be when nothing hurt any more. But she kept on hurting . . . and over the silliest of things. First the rose she'd thrown away, which she now had an inexpressible yearning for. Then over the things her hungry eyes had noticed about him, even though she'd spent most of the time trying not to look at him at all.

There was a small scar on his lower lip and another on his forehead that sliced through his right eyebrow. Old rugby injuries? Australian Rules Football? Boxing? Surfing?

To Laurel, looking for a cure for her misery and not finding it, it suddenly mattered a great deal that Connor had had thirty-five years of living that she knew nothing at all about, and was never likely to know. What had put the laughter lines around his eyes and the frown marks between his eyebrows? Had those lines on either side of his mouth been dimples before he'd grown from round-faced boyhood to lean, masculine maturity?

Were these the sort of question marks he'd been talking about? The terrible wanting to know all those things only a lover had business knowing? Was that why he'd been so sure, and she'd been so scared?

But she'd been entitled to be scared. She didn't

believe in love. Love needed trust to back it up, and she didn't have any. All she believed in was the fierceness of physical attraction that was bliss while it lasted and hell when it was over. She couldn't let herself in for that again.

She'd have to be sure, very sure, something more was on offer before she put herself at risk again. If she ever could. She'd become so very good at protecting herself, she didn't know how to stop. Besides, she had a lot more than herself to protect now. She had Lianne, whose precious little life no man must be allowed to disrupt.

And Connor would be disruptive, if she let him close enough. She'd only known him four days, he had no claim on her, but she still felt as if she'd been put through a mangle. It, this, Connor—whatever! —had to be stopped. But she'd already done that, hadn't she?

Laurel was still thinking of Connor when the motorway fed her into town and traffic closed around her. Connor and herself . . . herself and Connor . . . her mind went round and round as though it were trapped in a maze.

The truth, when she faced up to it, wasn't very comforting. Alan had crippled her emotions and she preferred to live with her injuries than face up to the cure . . . because she was very much afraid it wasn't a cure Connor offered, but a *coup de grâce*.

The flat smelled stale, airless, after being closed up for the weekend. Laurel flung open the windows until the cold made her close them again. She tried to lose herself in a flurry of chores, putting away the groceries she'd picked up at a store along the road, unpacking her weekend-bag, throwing her washing in the machine and tackling the ironing that had been waiting since last Thursday.

Eventually she thought about lunch but, although it was well into the afternoon, she wasn't hungry. She wouldn't let herself dwell on why, but switched on her answering maching. That cool, female voice from Dyson Enterprises (UK) Ltd reminded her of her afternoon appointment. As if she was likely to forget—but, of course, Connor hadn't known he would meet up with her that morning. He must have left prior instructions.

Laurel phoned Lianne for a chat, and then she called her building society to arrange an appointment for the following day to discuss a mortgage. After that she settled down to work out a new set of sums to see what sort of a deposit she could offer, although she couldn't be certain until she knew what her lease would fetch.

It was a very determined, very controlled Laurel who was searching for a parking space in Mayfair at a quarter-past four that afternoon. She eventually found one, walked through a fashionable square and along a side street. She was wearing a long, full-skirted, tight-belted, silver-grey raincoat with a dark grey silk scarf filling the open neckline.

For all her resolution, her heart skipped a beat when she saw Connor's car. It was parked outside a tall Georgian house which had only a discreet brass nameplate to show it was no longer a private residence. So he was here. So what? She was sure she'd become an embarrassment he'd want to avoid as much as she wanted to avoid him.

The brass handle on the front door turned to her touch, and she found herself in an entrance hall where eggshell-blue walls and a thick blue carpet kept up the impression of an elegant private house. Even the table that served as a reception desk was an elegant period piece.

The slender redheaded woman who rose to greet her gave her such an appraising look and said, 'Miss Curtis' with such certainty that Laurel instantly suspected Connor had arranged another little trap. Then she told herself to stop being silly, that any instructions he'd given would be to keep her out of his way.

She was led past a gracefully curving staircase to a door almost at the end of the passage. The receptionist opened it and slid back the metal door of a dainty cage-type lift that reminded Laurel of an old-fashioned hotel she'd once stayed in on a trip to Paris.

'Very French,' she murmured as she followed the receptionist in. There was just room for the two of them and they passed no other landings until the lift stopped.

The receptionist slid back the door of the lift, opened another door and they stepped out into a narrow passage carpeted in red. Laurel was mystified. They seemed to be at the top storey and the receptionist was leading her towards what must be the front of the house. She stopped opposite a narrow flight of stairs and pressed the bell on what looked very much like a front door.

Laurel had the sudden, horrible suspicion that this was a private flat above the offices, and she demanded, 'Who am I supposed to be seeing?'

At that moment the door opened and a stripe-suited man with a blissfully unknown face stood there. The receptionist said, 'Miss Curtis, this is our accountant, Mr Walton. Mr Walton, Miss Curtis.' She walked back to the lift and Laurel felt limp with relief as she shook hands with the accountant.

For a moment there she'd thought, she'd really thought . . .

One of her suspicions was correct, though, because she was led through a small hall into what was undoubtedly the sitting-room of a private flat, a beautifully preserved time-capsule of Regency elegance from around the time this house had been built.

Then the time-capsule burst, and with it Laurel's sense of security. Rising from one of two settees facing a sofa-table littered with papers was Connor Dyson.

CHAPTER FOUR

MR WALTON said, 'Let me take your coat, Miss Curtis. You've met Mr Dyson, I believe?'

'Yes,' Laurel replied, letting him take her coat but not extending her hand to Connor. He didn't seem to expect it, so why had he set up this intimate kind of meeting? Perhaps he wasn't the kind of man who took kindly to rejection. Perhaps he wanted some kind of revenge.

Laurel didn't want to think that of him, but he was certainly watching her warily. For all her misgivings, she was glad she was wearing a new, dusty-pink wool dress with a belt tied loosely below her slender waist. Her mother had sent it from Geneva, in one of those rare moments when she remembered she was a mother, and however unmaternal she might be she had excellent taste.

Laurel kept on her grey silk scarf and gloves to indicate she didn't expect to stay long, and Mr Walton invited her to sit opposite Connor, who waited until she was settled before sitting down again himself. Very polite, Laurel thought. Perhaps he was more civilised on his home ground. She thought of what he was like when he was less civilised and her pulses fluttered.

Before they had time to steady, the accountant said, 'I'll just see about the coffee,' and went out the way Laurel had just come in. She heard the front door close and, a little later, the clang of the metal lift.

'He's not coming back, is he?' she asked stonily.

'No.'

'And this is your flat, not your office.'

Connor didn't bother to deny it. 'I thought if we got the atmosphere right, we might still be friends.'

'I don't want to be friends.'

'Don't be childish, Laurie.'

With his lazy, Australian accent he could make the most outrageous things sound normal and pleasant. Laurel reacted angrily. 'You made a pass at me, which I didn't appreciate, so now I'm being childish? That's typical!'

She picked up her bag to leave, but he said calmly, 'You don't have to run away again. I'm not going to chase you around the room. I do learn, you know.'

Incredibly, he made her feel foolish, as though she was keeping up a feud he'd lost interest in. She *did* want to storm out, but she didn't want to be foolish. Besides, she had to know how much her lease was worth before she could arrange a mortgage.

For the moment, Connor had the upper hand. It was better to go along with him than risk a confrontation in which she could very well be worsted. Simmering with resentment, she leaned back, crossed her long legs and tried to look bored. Connor, however, didn't appear to notice. He was opening a file that had her name on it and taking out her lease. Then he put on a pair of horn-rimmed glasses.

Laurel was taken aback. Those riveting grey eyes that played such havoc with her senses were short-sighted. Hopelessly, helplessly, she was swamped with a tenderness for him that weakened her more than his physical magnetism.

Connor glanced at her, saw the way her eyes had softened and her lips had parted, and explained, 'For the small print.' Then he seemed to realise there was so much more than surprise on her face. His voice changed and he said, 'Laurie . . .?'

'I—I never thought of you as wearing glasses,' she managed lamely.

'I had the impression you never thought of me at all.' And he smiled.

That was Connor Dyson, she thought bitterly. A moment's weakness and he pounced. She should know better than to go all soft simply because he needed help with the small print. A panther would look endearing in glasses, but it wouldn't lessen its menace!

'The way I've been badgered about my lease, it would have been impossible not to think of you,' she retorted.

'Ah, the lease. I'm disappointed.' He returned his attention to the document. 'This lease was originally made out to Alan Curtis. A relation?'

'No. The surname was sheer coincidence.'

'Who was he, then?'

He was still digging for information he had no right to know. She could have told him so, but she had the urge to jolt him, if he could be jolted. 'A lover. He signed the lease over to me when we split up.'

Actually, that wasn't quite the way it had happened. She hadn't known they were splitting up. The lease was transferred into her name so she could sell it when he sent for her.

Alan had been working as a TV researcher at the time, waiting for a chance to get before the cameras. It had come when he'd been offered a trial by the owner of an American TV station who was looking for an English presenter for a news show.

'As soon as I get a permanent contract I'll send for you,' Alan had told her. 'If it doesn't work out, there'll still be the flat to come back to.'

He'd been in the States for a month when she'd phoned him with news too good to keep to herself. 'Alan, we're having a baby! Can you imagine it? Your brown eyes, my turned-up nose . . .'

'Laurel, we can't have a baby now. The timing's wrong,' Alan broke in.

'Tell that to the baby.' She was too deliriously happy to be on her guard. Why should she be? They were engaged and he was always telling her how much he loved her.

'I'm building a new career, Laurel. My image is important. A wife and child wouldn't do me any good. You'll have to get rid of it.'

Get rid of it. Their baby. Her world crashed and, from somewhere in the ruins, she told him, 'You'll have to give me a better reason than your image, Alan.'

Too late he remembered his charm, his voice deepening and caressing her from thousands of miles away. 'Laurel, darling, you're being over-emotional. Your career's at stake as well as mine.'

'I'm a writer, Alan. I can always earn. Maybe I'll turn to fiction. It's what I always intended, anyway.'

'Eventually, perhaps, but not now. You can scarcely be pregnant at all. Fix it now, before you get all maternal.'

She couldn't believe Alan could change so much in such a short time. There could only be one answer. 'There's somebody else, isn't there?'

Alan hesitated just long enough to confirm her suspicions before he said, 'Not really. Nobody that need affect us in the long run. It's just that Natalie has got a bit of a thing about me at the moment. I have to kid her along until I'm well enough established to do without her.'

Natalie? Laurel remembered she was the daughter of Alan's employer. He'd mentioned meeting her in London with her father, nothing more, but suddenly it wasn't so surprising he'd won the job against more experienced applicants. Laurel felt smirched as she realised this thing with Natalie must have started while he'd still been vowing undying love for her.

Alan must have found her silence encouraging because he went on, 'Check into a private clinic. I'll pay the bill and send you something extra to splurge on yourself. You were saying you needed new clothes . . .'

Laurel hung up. She was numb for a while, but eventually she realised that, although it might be possible to love and hate a man, it wasn't possible to love and despise him, and she despised Alan. He'd turned something she thought wonderful into something shoddy, and she couldn't forgive him for that.

All she was left with was a fierce protectiveness towards the baby, and she wanted it twice as much because he didn't. She'd had a lifetime of being unwanted herself, which she'd thought had ended when she'd met Alan. All that had really ended, as it turned out, was her belief in love.

She'd never contacted Alan again, and months later she learned on the grapevine that he'd married Natalie. It hadn't meant anything to her. She'd learned to cope all by herself, and she was still coping . . .

Connor asked, with an edge on his voice which she took to be irritation, 'Does the mention of Alan Curtis always put you in a trance?'

Laurel wondered how long she'd been staring at him and seeing instead the face of the man who'd taught her that, if she couldn't love wisely, it was better not to love at all. 'I'm sorry,' she apologised frigidly. 'Could we get back to the lease?'

'I never left it, you did.' Having made his point, Connor didn't push it, but went on, 'Right, this was one of the last seven-year leases issued. Curtis held it for over a year, transferred it to you, and there are still seventeen months to run. We would like you to move by the third of April, which leaves one year outstanding. All clear so far?'

Laurel nodded and Connor continued, 'Our standard offer for the surrender of a full year's lease is five thousand pounds, plus another two thousand to cover inconvenience, removals and improvements.' He referred to a note attached to the lease, and asked, 'Do you intend to take with you the storage heaters and shower fittings you've had installed?'

'No,' she replied, knowing she wouldn't need them at The Pantiles.

'In that case we offer an extra thousand in compensation. Is that satisfactory?'

'It's generous,' Laurel said, stunned. Eight thousand

pounds in all. If she put that down as a deposit with the money she'd saved over the past three years, the mortgage repayments would be within her scope when she took a lower-paid, provincial job. And she still had five months' London earnings to come, which would make a useful contingency fund if anything went wrong. She wouldn't be able to save much, if anything, once she took on the house. She'd have an au pair to support, as well as herself and Lianne.

She was so relieved, she admitted, 'It's much more than I expected. I couldn't hope to get anywhere near that on the open market with the state Hewitt House is in now.'

'We took that into account, since the current "state" is our responsibility.' Connor dropped his formality, and asked, 'You sure you're satisfied?'

'I'm delighted.'

'You don't want to make any additional claims?'

'No.'

'Then what was the point of holding out so long?'

'I wasn't holding out. I'm a freelance journalist,' Laurel explained. 'I fix up my shifts for the week every Thursday, but sometimes I'm offered additional shifts or assignments. That's when I have to cancel other things.'

'It's a bit precarious, isn't it? Freelancing?'

'It was at first, but now I'm well-established. I earn more this way than if I took a staff job. Even before your company bought Hewitt House I didn't intend to stay there all my life.' Suddenly Laurel realised they were talking in a natural, friendly manner, and that made her nervous. 'Is there a surrender of the lease document you want me to sign?'

Connor put two forms in front of her. 'One copy for you, one for us. When you've read them through, here's where to sign.' He came round to her side of the sofa-table and leaned over her, flicking through the pages and pointing. 'Here, here and here. All right?'

Laurel nodded, overpoweringly conscious of his closeness, and the worst part of it was that some weakness within her wanted him close. She was both glad and sorry when he straightened up and stepped away.

He put his glasses down on the table and said, 'I'll see to the coffee now.'

'Ah, yes, the coffee,' she murmured. 'Has poor Mr Walton got back from Brazil with the beans?'

Connor smiled, and Laurel's uncertain heart was squeezed again. 'Don't worry about Robbie,' he told her. 'We're getting on fine. I may not know much about finesse, but you must admit I'm on my best behaviour. It's safe to take off your gloves and scarf, promise!'

He left her feeling foolish, as he so often did, and she watched him go through a door at the back of the sitting-room, which she supposed must lead to the kitchen. Ruefully she slipped off her scarf and gloves, thinking Connor Dyson would be a man she could like if only she wasn't so afraid of becoming involved with him. She looked at his glasses on the table and her fingers strayed towards them with a yearning that was really for the man himself. She allowed herself to touch them, then snatched her hand away and picked up the first of the documents.

Laurel forced herself to read it through carefully, every last legal clause, just to make sure she knew exactly what she was signing. It was all part of trusting nobody but herself. Her eyes strayed to Connor's glasses. Her instincts told her she could trust him, but what did her instincts know? She'd trusted Alan, too.

She preferred to trust her brain now. Connor couldn't confuse that, provided she kept him at a safe distance. She skimmed through the second document to make sure it was an exact copy, and when he came back she said, 'I'm ready to sign.'

He put the coffee-tray on a bow-fronted Sheraton sideboard, came over and sat beside her, unnecessarily close. He gave her his pen and leaned forward with her as she prepared to sign. She was so disconcerted, she said, 'Don't you need your glasses?'

'Not to sign my name. I told you, only for the small print. Why, do my glasses bother you?'

Their faces were turned towards each other and she was nervous enough to be honest. 'I feel safer when you're wearing your glasses.'

'I must be slipping,' Connor murmured. 'You should never feel safe with me. I never feel safe with you.'

Laurel moved away from him. 'You just told me——'

'So I did. Sorry. Back to best behaviour, Laurie. Promise.'

'You're very good with promises,' she grumbled, signing her name in the three stipulated places, 'and my name's Laurel.'

'I prefer Laurie, but I'll call you Laurel if you call me

Connor. So far you've avoided calling me anything. Is it a deal?'

She nodded, albeit grudgingly, and he smiled and added his signature to the document. She studied it. Flamboyant, just as she'd supposed. They signed the second document as well, and whenever he took the pen from her he somehow or other managed to caress her fingers, sending tingling sensations all over her.

Did he know what he was doing to her? Was it deliberate? Even when she managed a surreptitious glance at his face she couldn't be sure. She only knew he seemed formal again as her gave her the copy of the document and took a cheque from the folder.

'Half the agreed sum is payable on signature to help you get resettled,' he told her. 'The other half will be paid when you vacate the flat. Would you like to use the scheme we've set up to help people find other accommodation?'

'No, thank you.'

Connor frowned. 'You sure you're not being proud?'

'Why should you say that?'

'You strike me as a very proud person.'

'It's amazing what you find in Hewitt House, isn't it?' Laurel replied lightly. 'If it makes you feel better, I'm not too proud to accept that cup of coffee.'

Connor stood up and his careful good humour seemed to have left him. 'If you think I'm trying to put you under some sort of obligation to me, I'm not.'

'Fair enough.' She didn't like the baffled way he looked at her, and pretended not to notice by adding, 'No milk and one sugar, please.'

He continued looking at her for several seconds, then

turned away to the coffee-tray. Laurel seized the
opportunity to move further along the settee. He must
have noticed. When he sat down after giving her a cup
of coffee, he didn't try to crowd her.

'It's a lovely flat,' she said conversationally.

'I bought it as it stands with the house.' He didn't
seem interested. 'Have dinner with me tonight,
Laurie.'

His sudden change of tack took her by surprise. 'I'm
working tonight. Six until one in the morning.'

She looked at her watch and he said irritably, 'You're
always doing that.'

Laurel put down her cup. 'If we're going to start
quarrelling again . . .'

'No.' He reached out and touched her arm briefly.
'I'm sorry. What about lunch in Paris tomorrow? I'm
flying by private charter for a business meeting. I could
pick you up at nine and have you back by five.'

Lunch in Paris, just like that. To live irresponsibly
just for one day . . . to have fun without counting the
consequences . . . what bliss that would be. Laurel was
sorely, sorely tempted and Connor knew it. 'What are
you hesitating for?' he asked. 'You want to come.'

Laurel stood up and went over to the mantelpiece,
ostensibly to study a piece of Meissen porcelain, but in
fact to buy time. She wanted so much to say yes, but
she had to shake her head. 'I've got a business meeting,
too.'

'Cancel it.'

She looked quizzically over her shoulder at him.
'Your meeting is important but mine isn't? That's
typical, too.'

Connor came over to her, took the figurine, put it back on the mantelpiece and held on to her hand. 'I didn't mean it like that. I meant my meeting would get us both to Paris for lunch. That's what's important to me.'

She slipped her hand out of his, knowing she was never going to make a rational decision while he was touching her. 'It isn't just that. I don't want to find myself a snippet in the gossip columns.'

'That rubbish!' Connor scoffed. 'Ignore it. I do.'

'We're living in different worlds. Mine's private. I like it that way.' Laurel moved along the fireplace, trying unobtrusively to put some space between them. 'I don't want to get caught up in your playboy image.'

Connor's eyes gleamed. 'Is that why you won't have anything to do with me? Because of some stupid image cooked up by gossip columnists?' He saw the way Laurel raised her eyebrows and went on, 'All right, I'll admit I don't live like a monk, but there's nobody special in my life.'

I wonder, Laurel thought, if Lady Letitia knows that?

'Apart,' Connor continued deliberately, 'from you—and will you stop looking at that bloody watch?'

He sounded so savage that Laurel jumped. It had been a nervous reaction, looking at her watch, because when Connor turned on the charm she didn't know how to counter it. She was so vulnerable with him, she forgot all her flip retorts. 'I'm sorry, but I have to work tonight. I've got time for one more coffee and that's about it.'

She saw the effort he was making to keep his

temper, and thought she wasn't going to get away with it, but eventually he said, 'All right, but you come with me to make it.'

He took her wrist and pulled her into the kitchen. He switched on the percolator without letting her go, and she protested, 'You've left the cups in the sitting-room.'

'Damn the cups. Damn everything until you agree to come out with me. If not tomorrow, then Wednesday. I'm not letting you go until you do.'

He meant it, no doubt about that. Half of Laurel was thrilled, the other half wanted a place to hide. Her indecision made her angry. 'Great,' she told him sullenly. 'This way I end up with a matching set of bruises.'

Then she wished she'd kept quiet, because he lifted her wrist and kissed it, sending delicious tremors all over her nervous system. She looked around frantically—for what she didn't know—and saw a champagne glass half-filled with water. Propped in it was a short-stemmed, yellow rose.

'Connor, you saved my rose!' She couldn't believe this unpredictable caveman had a soft and romantic streak.

He glowered at her, embarrassed. 'I didn't see why it should end up under a truck just because you didn't want it.'

'But I did. I was so sorry I threw it away.'

Connor looked at her carefully, weighing up whether she meant it. He decided she did and reached for the rose. He wiped the wet stem on his shirt and offered it to her.

Laurel looked at it with misty eyes. The rose was a little battered, but that only made it more precious. She looked at the damp patch on Connor's shirt, and realised that made him more precious, too. She was going quietly crazy and it was bliss.

It seemed so obvious now that since exchanging that first look with Connor she'd been running a race that couldn't be won, no matter how hard she tried. She couldn't run any more, so she had to trust . . .

She tilted her face up to his, her fair hair falling back from her shoulders. Her eyes were soft and shining, her voice husky as she reminded him, 'It goes behind the ear, I believe.'

Carefully, as though he couldn't believe the battle was won, Connor slotted the rose into place. Laurel smiled and he breathed, 'Heaven knows, I've waited long enough for you to smile at me, but it was worth it, Laurie.'

She didn't tell him it was only four days, or that her name was Laurel. She was learning the strength of his arms around her, the feel of her body against his, and watching his lips coming down to smother hers.

CHAPTER FIVE

CONNOR'S first kiss drew the soul from her body. She melted against him, reassured that they were brought together by more than a physical flame that could die as quickly as it flared. She wanted to put her head on his shoulder and cling to him while she got used again to being to being a proper woman, alive and vulnerable.

Connor didn't give her the time she needed. He pressed scorching kisses on her face and neck, his hands moving over her body with a hunger she wasn't ready for. He seemed to be devouring her, sweeping away her first protests with an ardour that all but overpowered her.

Laurel began to struggle in earnest, but he didn't seem to notice. He was out of control, pursuing the sensation of the moment while she, who'd reached out tentatively for love, was getting a mauling. What little trust she'd managed to scrape together fled. She wanted to weep, she felt so cheated.

Connor found the zip at the back of her dress and jerked it down. The soft material slid from her shoulder and his lips fastened on her softer flesh. Laurel gasped. It sounded more like a gasp of ecstasy than of anguish, but this wasn't what she wanted. She was weakening fast and he was so strong. She used the last of her strength to put her hands against his chest and strain away from him.

At last he realised she meant it. He didn't let her go, but his arms loosened. He raised his head and said thickly, 'What is it, Laurie?'

What could she say? That she'd thought the feeling between them went deeper than sexual need? How pathetic she would sound, how unbelievably naïve. He would laugh at her and she couldn't bear that. She'd already lost her hopes and her dignity; she had no intention of losing her pride.

'I have to go to work.' She twisted out of his arms, pulling her dress together and reaching with trembling fingers round the back to zip it up.

'Work?' Connor stared at her blankly.

'Yes, work.' She tried to sound as decisive as usual, and hoped her shaking legs would hold up long enough to get her out of his house and his life.

He caught her arm and swung her round to face him. 'You mean that's it? You get me in this state and then walk out on me? There are names for girls like you!'

She could have told him there were names for men like him, and other things beside, but she couldn't find the words. He must have found her silence damning, because he went on bitterly, 'I hope you've had your fun. I only wish I could say it's been a pleasure.'

He let go of her contemptuously and, as he did so, he caught sight of the rose that had fallen from her hair. His foot went over it and he ground it into the floor. 'That's the end of that little game. The next time you feel like playing, pick on somebody else.'

His unfairness smote her. If it was a game, he'd started it, and it wasn't her fault if she'd been playing by a different set of rules. She stumbled out of the kitchen into the sitting-room, threw on her coat and grabbed her scarf, bag and gloves from the settee.

When she got to the front door he already had it open. He was leaning against it, arms folded, watching her sweep past him with a bitter contempt that made a mockery of the light she had once seen in his eyes.

I offered an inch, she thought, he took a mile, so it's all my fault. It must be the injustice that was making her eyes smart. Connor Dyson certainly wasn't worth it.

Laurel didn't bother with the lift. She headed straight for the stairs. At one time this must have been the servants' quarters. The stairs were steep and narrow, and they kept turning on themselves. She wasn't seeing too straight so she stumbled more than once before she came out on to a broad, blue-carpeted passage that led to the wide, gracefully curving staircase she'd noticed from the hall.

She hurried down it, half fearful he would come after her with more abuse. When she rushed through the hall the receptionist looked up with startled eyes. I must look as if I've been dragged through a hedge backwards, Laurel thought, and then it occurred to her that the receptionist—like the accountant—must have been in on Connor's little conspiracy.

Everything had been stacked against her from the start, just the way he'd planned it, and her cheeks flamed as she recalled how nearly, and how willingly, she'd fallen into the trap. But she didn't blame him. She blamed herself for being stupid enough to do what she'd vowed she'd never do—put her trust in him. It was a mistake she wouldn't be making again.

Ironically, Laurel was back in Mayfair that night. She was parked outside the home of a city financier rumoured to be at the centre of a gigantic fraud. It was doubtful if he'd return home at all, but her job was to wait and watch, just in case.

It was a dull job for a night when she needed movement, excitement, anything that would take her mind off Connor. That ugly, hateful scene hadn't killed the feeling she had for him, as she was only too miserably aware. Nothing had changed, except that she felt stricken and more afraid of him than ever.

She wasn't recalled to the newsroom until eleven and she made a slight detour to pass Connor's house. The lights were on at the top. So he was home. She didn't know what good that did her, because if he'd been standing outside the front door she'd only have shot straight past.

Laurel knew she was showing all the symptoms of love, but she also knew how deceptive symptoms could be. The sickness could be something different entirely—pure physical attraction, as Connor had decided. If she'd had his honesty she could be cured by now. It was a troubling thought to take back to the newsroom with her.

She wasn't sent out again, and when she drove home at one in the morning she might have been the only person still awake in the slumbering city, an illusion she normally enjoyed. Tonight, however, she just felt lonely.

She was locking up her car outside Hewitt House when she thought she heard another car door shut. It was quietly done, but she was always on the alert until she reached the safety of her flat. She straightened and stared along the line of parked cars.

In a pool of darkness between two street lamps she saw a burly, darker shape moving towards her. Laurel sprinted for the doors of Hewitt House, leaping up the shallow steps. Her hand was on the handle when she heard, 'Laurie!'

Only one person called her that and, besides, the accent was unmistakable. Her heart thudded with a different fear. She slipped inside the doors and reached in the darkness for the light switch. Only one of the two low-watt economy bulbs came on, but it was something. She hurried along the narrow hall. She'd almost reached the stairs when the doors opened and closed behind her and she heard Connor say again, 'Laurie.'

She stopped without turning to face him. His hand touched her shoulder. When she jumped, it was just as quickly removed. He said awkwardly, 'I didn't mean to frighten you. I just came to say sorry . . . for rushing you, for the things I said. I didn't mean any of it.'

Bitterness gave Laurel the courage to turn and face him. 'You did.'

Connor shook his head. 'I knew I'd wrecked it. I was so mad, I turned my anger on you. I can only explain it by saying I've never felt that you and I were strangers. That's crazy if you like, but I felt it so deeply that the preliminaries didn't seem necessary.'

Laurel had never heard anything so arrogant in all her life, and her bitterness increased. 'You mean if you'd taken me out to dinner first that would have given you the right to strip me?'

'No! If you'll listen for a minute——'

His vehemence made Laurel back away and she broke in angrily, 'No, you listen! You own this building, so I can't very well keep you out of it, but it's also my home. If you have any respect for me, you'll also respect my privacy—and leave me alone.'

She turned and plunged up the stairs. It seemed that finally she'd got through to him, because he didn't try to follow her. When she got to her flat, she closed the front door behind her and leaned against it, trying to pull herself together.

She remembered telling him what time she finished work, but she couldn't comprehend what had driven him here with an apology, and an explanation even he admitted was crazy. Or was it? Had he been compelled to come here, just as she'd been compelled to drive past his house earlier?

It was a romantic notion, but Laurel told herself she was not a romantic. If she'd gone soft on Connor it was, as he'd proved so forcefully, merely physical; if she'd also gone soft on a certain yellow rose, she'd seen with her own eyes what had happened to it. She'd done herself and the rose no good at all.

Then she found herself wondering why Connor had saved the rose in the first place. It certainly hadn't been for effect, because he'd hidden it in the kitchen and been embarrassed about it. The man was an enigma. So primitive and obvious one minute, so covertly romantic the next.

And then she thought she knew why he was still chasing her. To him, she must be an enigma, too—and he was a man who hated question marks. He'd said so himself. There must be a big question mark over her head. What a challenge that must be to a man who was used to getting what he wanted!

A shiver that might have been a thrill ran down her spine. If Connor was hunting her in earnest, he wouldn't give up. He would continue tracking her until he had her trapped.

Impatiently, Laurel checked her thoughts. They were running so wild, they were becoming ridiculous. Yet as she prepared for bed it seemed even more ridiculous not to be wary of whatever Connor did next. Unless she wanted to be caught . . .

Laurel slept fitfully, awoke unrefreshed and heavy-eyed. She had tea and toast, but she was so much on edge that she decided to change her normal routine and go jogging before she did anything else. The uneasy feeling that she was trying to run away from herself persisted, but she told herself wryly that it made a change from running away from Connor.

She put on her yellow track-suit and trainers, tied her hair in a pony-tail and ran down the stairs with a lightness that belied her heavy heart. She could hear noises that suggested there were workmen somewhere in the building, and supposed another flat was being boarded up.

It wasn't until she reached the hall that she saw the workmen, and then only incidentally, because standing there looking as bronzed and vital as the first time she'd seen him was Connor.

Laurel's steps faltered. He wasn't even supposed to be in London. Lunch in Paris, she remembered with a pang. George the caretaker was with him, and he, Connor and the workmen all seemed to see her at the same time.

Work ceased and Connor said formally, 'Good morning, Miss Curtis. I hope we haven't disturbed you. I had the work delayed specially.'

Dumbfounded, she shook her head.

Connor glanced at the workmen. They hurriedly returned to work and he went on, 'I'm having those useless front doors replaced with heavy security ones.'

Laurel found her tongue and, thinking how few tenants still remained, she said, 'It's a bit late in the day, isn't it?'

'I didn't realise how vulnerable this building was until I looked in unexpectedly last night, and I believe in protecting my property, however late.'

He was still so formal, but were his grey eyes telling her she was the one who was vulnerable and in need of protection? Her heart contracted. What a delicious luxury it would be to know somebody was looking after her. Then she remembered she'd warned herself to be wary of another approach from Connor, and this, surely, was the cleverest one of all.

'You'll be given a set of keys,' he went on. 'The lighting will be improved and kept on all night. If you have any problems I haven't thought of, tell George and they'll be seen to right away.'

Because she couldn't help herself, Laurel said, 'You were supposed to be in Paris today.'

Then she wished she'd kept quiet, because George was looking from one to the other of them with undisguised interest. Connor must have been conscious of it, too, for he replied blandly, 'I had more important things to see to. The meeting's postponed until tomorrow, and all other possible arrangements are postponed with it.'

Was that his oblique way of telling her lunch in Paris was still on if she was interested? He had a nerve, but then she'd always known that, hadn't she? 'I hope you enjoy yourself,' she said, and left him standing there.

She ran her usual course along the streets and around the park without knowing much about it. When she got back, Connor had gone. She'd been dreading another encounter but, denied it, she felt more depressed than ever. Perhaps he'd guessed she would. For somebody she'd accused of lacking finesse, he was a pretty shrewd operator.

Just *how* shrewd she discovered when she reached the top storey and found an oblong Cellophane-wrapped box outside her door. Inside was a beautiful yellow rose. Laurel knew that if she had any sense she'd jump on it. Instead, she picked it up and carried it into her flat.

It was a long time since anybody had sent her a hothouse rose, and she had to search her kitchen cupboards for a tall, slim vase to put it in. Then she spent several seconds looking at the rose, anything to delay opening the little envelope that accompanied it.

The flower she could appreciate. The card, she sensed, she probably wouldn't. Eventually curiosity drove her to tear open the envelope. There wasn't the usual card inside, but a note. She recognised the flamboyant writing immediately, and with a wildly skipping heart she read, 'I've done my best, but I still won't feel you're really safe until you're with me. That's my private number below. Please phone. Connor.'

So the new security doors were for her. Laurel cynically decided that she wasn't being so much cherished as impressed. She couldn't think of anybody she was less safe with than Connor Dyson.

She screwed up the note and threw it in the bin. Five minutes later she rescued it, smoothed it out and put it in her dressing-table drawer. She could forget it there, she told herself, as much as anywhere else. But she had to practically sit on her hands to keep them away from the telephone, and she was glad when the time came to fix up her mortgage.

She had no problems there, but when she came out she didn't feel like skipping down the street, and she should have. She'd worked so long and so hard for a proper home for herself and Lianne, and she'd done it all by herself. She was entitled to a sense of achievement.

Instead, she felt deflated. It was only when she was driving to work that evening that she was honest enough with herself to admit why. Connor had knocked her world off-centre, distorting her aims and ambitions. She couldn't get excited about anything that didn't include him.

That made her feel terribly guilty about Lianne. Laurel wondered miserably where all the guilt came from. For three and a half years she'd been feeling guilty about working away from Lianne so she could provide properly for them both, now she was feeling guilty because being with her full time no longer seemed enough.

The more she pushed Connor away, the more he pressed in on her. She was obsessed with him, but she knew him well enough by now to realise that if she let him into her life he would take over. She couldn't give that sort of commitment. It wouldn't only open her own life to disruption, but Lianne's as well. She couldn't let that happen. She remembered only too well the disruptions she'd suffered when she'd been little.

What was the answer, then? Work, Laurel decided. Keep herself so busy that Connor was kept out. She normally worked one double shift a week to boost her income—doing a day shift on one paper, the night shift on another and sleeping through until the next night's shift came up. In future she would do two. She could manage if she spaced them three days apart, and there would be so much less time to think. Under those conditions she'd forget Connor quickly enough.

Unfortunately, she reckoned without Connor. He wouldn't let himself be forgotten. Every morning there was a beautifully packaged yellow rose on her doorstep. On Friday she phoned him. Perversely, she used his office number, not his personal one. She was put through so quickly, she wondered uneasily whether his entire staff knew what was—or wasn't—going on between her and their boss.

Laurel didn't beat about the bush. 'Connor, stop sending me roses. You're embarrassing me.'

'I'll stop if you'll let me come and see you.'

'No!'

'Come and see me, then.'

'No.'

'Then expect more roses,' Connor said. 'At least they've got you talking to me. This respecting your privacy is killing me.'

Laurel hung up.

The next morning there wasn't a single rose on her doorstep, there was a bunch of a dozen, and so there was every morning afterwards. By Tuesday Laurel felt she was living in a florist's and phoned again. When she heard that confident voice say 'Dyson', she didn't bandy words. She just said, 'Connor . . . please . . .' and put the phone down.

It worked. There were no roses the next day. Everywhere Laurel looked in her flat there were roses, and the only ones she wanted were the ones she didn't get.

As soon as she got up on Thursday she looked outside her door. Still no roses. The siege, it seemed, was over. Connor had taken her at her word at last.

She wished he hadn't.

At work that night she had an overwhelming urge to hear his voice, even if it was only saying 'Dyson' one more time. She resisted the urge to phone him until nine o'clock, then she ran out of resistance. It would, she decided, only be civil to thank him for being co-operative.

She used his personal number, and she was as nervous

as a kitten while she waited for him to answer. What if he saw through her politeness and started gloating? She would die of embarrassment. Well, she could always hang up. She was pretty good at that.

The voice that said 'hello' was female.

Laurel's heart constricted. 'Who am I speaking to?' she asked.

'Letitia Hinds. Do you want Connor?'

'No,' Laurel replied remotely. 'I'm sorry, I have the wrong number.' She put the phone down. So the siege, the roses, had meant nothing. She'd been nothing more than an ego trip for Connor; and his ego, it seemed, could stand only so much. She'd held out longest, so she'd won.

Laurel found no comfort in being the victor, and precious little in work, either, although she piled it on. She worked Friday night, did a day shift on Saturday and fell into bed on Saturday night exhausted, finally defeating the nervous energy that had kept her so hyped up.

She awoke a little before midday, feeling as hung-over as if she'd been to an all-night party that had lasted a week. That was all right, she didn't have to rush around. There was only the charity rugby match this afternoon. She didn't have to work again until tomorrow.

Superficially she looked the same bright-eyed, healthy Laurel as she drove to the rugby ground that afternoon, although the signs of stress were there. She'd lost a little weight, all of it apparently from her face, and there were mauve smudges under her eyes. She'd done a clever disguising job with make-up, a little blusher here, a little cover-up fluid there. Shrewd-eyed Aunt Sue would have noticed the difference in a flash, but she doubted if anyone else would.

The match had received a lot of publicity, mostly centred on the glamour girls playing for the Celebrities, and there was a fair-sized crowd when Laurel arrived. She parked and walked towards the sports pavilion, looking lithe and leggy in tight jeans, calf-hugging boots and a navy anorak. It was a cold, dry day, but the grass was waterlogged after days of rain.

Ahead of her, tottering on ridiculously high heels, was a small, slight figure she couldn't possibly mistake. 'Shirley,' she called, breaking into a run.

Shirley Dixon looked round, slipped, and Laurel just managed to grab her before she fell into the mud. Her diminutive ex-flatmate was wearing a fluffy white coat and hat, her pretty face was exquisitely made-up and her long, jade ear-rings were swaying madly after her near fall.

'Where do you think you're going—a cocktail party?' Laurel asked in amusement as she helped her across the grass.

'There's supposed to be a bit of a bash afterwards,' Shirley replied, picking her way delicately around a puddle.

'Afterwards? You don't mean you're playing? I thought your idea of exercise was limited to a cocktail shaker.'

'Generally speaking, yes, but I had a look at the list of sponsors and got my magazine to sponsor me. There are some useful contacts among them, not to say the occasional rich bachelor. I'm not wearing my jade for nothing.'

'You never change, Shirley.'

'I wish I could say the same for you. You used to leave me standing when it came to fun.' Shirley breathed a sigh of relief as she stepped off the grass on to the pavilion stairs and gave Laurel a searching look. 'How's Lianne?'

'Growing like mad. I'm buying The Pantiles in February, and putting out feelers for a job on a county paper.'

'So you finally earned enough, and not a moment too soon by the looks of you. Ease up, darling, you're not made of iron. Ring me when you're free for lunch. You need a rattling good lecture, better still a good man!'

Laurel pulled Shirley's hat down over her eyes and, laughing, they went into the changing-room, where there was a lot more laughter. When everybody was changed into their purple and white kits they were sorted into a team by Trisha Peters who was that rare bird, a female sports reporter.

Laurel found herself relaxing. It was impossible to be miserable in this crowd. She found she was down as fly-half, which was ironic, because that was the position Alan used to play. At least she knew something about it, which was more than Shirley, scrum-half because of her size, did.

When the two teams ran out on the pitch they were greeted with whistles and catcalls, most of which urged them to 'show a leg', which none of them could help doing anyway in their skimpy shorts. The Celebrities got all the attention from the cameras as they lined up for the start.

The match was never meant to be anything more than

a giggle to raise money for charity, and Laurel could never remember laughing so much in all her life—especially as she repeatedly picked Shirley out of the mud—but like the rest of her team she couldn't help playing to win. On the rare occasions Shirley got the ball out of the scrum and passed to her, she raced down the pitch, long legs flying, and scored three tries.

Not that the Ladies of the Press had everything their own way. A few of the Celebrities were athletes and they couldn't help playing to win, either. One girl who was playing in earnest and always getting in Laurel's way was a tall, slender brunette with a cheeky, kittenish face and hair cropped into a mop of dark curls.

The match was almost over when Laurel found herself clutching the slippery ball again. She took off down the pitch close to the line of spectators. She saw the tall brunette coming at her and just managed to pass the ball to Trisha before she was seized around the hips and brought crashing down.

She was under the brunette and they slid over the line into the spectators. Laurel lay there, tasting blood and mud, while she checked her teeth. They were all right. She must have bitten her lip. Somebody was lifting the brunette off her. Laurel heard her laugh and say, 'Trust it to be you, Connor. Always around when I need you.'

It couldn't be. Laurel raised her head and looked straight into the grey eyes that haunted her dreams and turned her days into a nightmare of longing. Connor was steadying the brunette with one arm, but he reached with the other to help Laurel. She glared at him, ignored his hand, got to her feet and ran back on to the pitch, wiping her bleeding lip on her sleeve.

Now she knew who the brunette was. Lady Letitia Hinds, estranged wife of Aussie racing driver Carlton Hinds, an Olympics skiing hope and current *amour* of Connor Dyson. And she looked so nice, damn her.

Connor must have been in the crowd all the time and she hadn't known it. Thank heavens for that. As it was, the brief respite from heartache was over, all her enjoyment gone. She was glad when the final whistle went a few minutes later and she was able to troop with the others into the haven of the changing room.

'I survived!' Shirley was crowing under the shower. 'Bring on the champers and the fellers.'

Laurel's full lower lip was the only injury of the day. Trisha put something on it that stung like mad but stopped the bleeding. When they'd all showered and changed back into their clothes, Trisha led them out of the changing room. Laurel was dreading the party, dreading seeing Connor with Lady Letitia.

Yet if she tried to excuse herself it would only bring on her the kind of notice she was anxious to avoid. Far better, she decided, to go in with her friends, mingle for a few minutes and slip away when nobody was watching.

But when she went into the clubhouse she found Connor had positioned himself where he could watch the door. Their eyes met, and he came towards her in that purposeful way she loved and dreaded.

CHAPTER SIX

THE CLUBHOUSE was packed with organisers, sponsors, celebrities, reporters and photographers. There was hardly room to breathe. Laurel's group was fragmenting, merging with the crowd. Only Shirley remained with her, and she was too small to hide behind.

Then Connor was before her, as solid and immovable as a brick wall. He was carrying two glasses of champagne. He put one in her hand, took her arm and began to steer her towards a wall where the crowd was thinner. He didn't notice Shirley at all.

'Connor!' Laurel protested, throwing an anguished glance back at Shirley, whose startled eyebrows had disappeared into her curly fringe.

'Ssh.' Connor's head bent over hers and for an outraged second she thought he kissed her hair. 'Wait until I find a quiet corner.'

Amazingly, he did find one. He edged her into it and stood squarely in front of her, blocking out the room entirely.

'Connor . . . please . . .' she begged.

'The last time you said that, I listened. I thought you might be pleased enough with me to phone. It's hell waiting for a call that never comes, Laurie.'

His directness took her aback. Defensively she exclaimed, 'I phoned you Thursday night! Lady

Letitia answered so I hung up.'

Connor's eyes gleamed and he definitely dropped a kiss on her hair. 'You didn't have to hang up. Were you jealous?'

'No, and don't kiss me like that.'

'I'm trying to show you there's no need to be jealous.'

'I wasn't! I was tactful. Unlike you, I don't enjoy embarrassing people. For heaven's sake, go back to Lady Letitia before she comes looking for you. This place is full of reporters, and I don't want them getting confused about who your latest "item" is. I told you, I value my privacy.'

Connor put a hand on the wall behind her and leaned closer still. 'You mustn't worry about Letty. We see each other occasionally and that's as far as it goes. Her husband Carl is a fellow Aussie. I was his best man when they married.'

'How cosy,' Laurel cooed. 'And how convenient now that they're divorcing.'

'Cut that out, Laurie,' Connor told her roughly. 'The divorce is a bloody tragedy. It's the papers that are making hay out of it, not me. What sort of a bloke do you think I am?'

'You've given me a very good demonstration, remember!'

'What do I have to do, walk on my knees to China?'

'Don't be ridiculous!' she snapped.

'You're the one who's being ridiculous. I made a mistake, I said I'm sorry. It won't happen again. What else do I have to do?'

'You could leave me alone.'

Connor tipped her face up to his and his grey eyes bored into hers. 'Do you really mean that?'

Laurel's eyes wavered and fell away. She'd just discovered she couldn't lie when he was looking at her like that. He pressed home his advantage immediately. 'Last Monday I waited two hours in the motorway café *willing* you to turn up. The waitress remembered me, and the rose, and she knew who I was waiting for. She felt very sorry for me. I felt very sorry for myself. You would have, too, if you'd shown up.'

'Oh.' Laurel was too female not to soften. 'I only go home the last weekend in the month. Sometimes I pop down for a few hours in between, but not regularly.'

Connor smiled. 'That makes me feel better. Will you feel better if I tell you you're the reason I came back to town today instead of tomorrow? I'm one of Letty's sponsors, but it was your name on the list of players that brought me here. I couldn't tell you what the game was like. I've only been watching you. It's the most pleasure I've had in a bloody awful week.'

Laurel felt the last of her resistance crumbling and bit her lip. Instantly his fingers touched it. 'Don't do that. It's hurt already. You practically did it at my feet. You'll never know how much I wanted to kiss you better, or how I felt when you looked at me that way.'

'I'm surprised you noticed. You had your arms full of Letty at the time.'

'Love you when you're jealous, Laurie,' he said softly.

'I'm not jealous!'

Laurel felt she was being hounded round in circles. Wearily she leaned her head against his shoulder for a moment in near defeat. 'I don't know what to do about you,' she admitted. 'All my instincts tell me you're trouble, and I don't have the time or energy for trouble.'

'We'll use my time and my energy.' His big hand came up to hold her head against him, very gently, very comfortingly, so that she almost relaxed into staying as she was.

Then she remembered how swift he was to pounce on a moment's weakness, and straightened up sharply. She sipped her champagne, thinking deeply, and eventually decided that, if she couldn't beat his directness, she could try to match it. 'Connor, what is all this? The old hunter's instinct? I'm running, so you can't help chasing?'

'If that's all it is, Laurie, I wouldn't be half so worried.'

He'd trumped her again. She raised troubled eyes to his and struggled on, 'Connor, I've already told you there's no room for a man in my life. I'm not playing or teasing, I mean it.'

His hand reached out to smooth away the furrow between her eyebrows. 'Come out to dinner with me this evening. If I can't make room for myself, I'll quit.'

'Honestly?' When he nodded, she added, 'Well, nowhere fashionable. I——'

'I know, you're paranoid about your privacy,' he broke in. 'I know a nice little pub in Surrey. It's quiet, the food is excellent, and you'll be the only reporter there. I'll pick you up at seven.'

'Make it eight. I have things to do first.'

'On a Sunday?' he asked sceptically.

'I've taken the day off, and my days off are always busy catching up on things I haven't had time for when I'm working. Tenants in Hewitt House don't run to maids, you know.'

'I could have you out of there tomorrow if you'd say the word.'

'Thanks, but I value my independence as much as my privacy,' she retorted swiftly.

'There would be no strings, just a better flat in a better area at a rent you can afford.'

'Connor,' she warned, 'if you try to reorganise my life, you won't see me for dust.'

He looked at her long and hard. Apparently he decided she meant it, because he just said, 'Until tonight at eight, then.'

Laurel gave him her champagne glass, nodded, and slipped away.

At seven o'clock that evening, Laurel, still glowing from a shower, was sitting on her bed, blow-drying her hair. She was also trying to quell her rising excitement, telling herself Connor's ability to lay on the charm with a trowel was as suspect as his determination to date her.

A man would go to almost any lengths to restore a dented ego, particularly if, like Connor, he was used to winning. She would have to let him down so lightly that somehow or other he felt honour had been restored. She would be gently negative, avoiding arguments that ignited the antagonism between them, steering him away from questions she didn't want to answer, and generally being so boring, he would be as relieved as she when the evening was over.

She might just manage it, she reckoned, if she could stay out of his reach. Connor liked touching her and, when he touched, her mind-over-matter philosophy melted with all the rest of her. So she not only had to be negative and evasive, she also had to be remote.

With Connor, that seemed a tall order.

Laurel switched off the hairdryer and stopped lecturing herself. She'd manage, simply because she had to, and she wasn't going to be sabotaged by this heady sense of anticipation that was racing through her nervous system like champagne.

There was a knock on the front door and she jumped. A glance at her watch on the bedside-table showed her it was almost an hour too early for Connor. She knotted her white towelling robe more securely around her waist and padded barefoot to the door, opening it as far as the chain would allow.

Connor stood there with a bunch of roses. He smiled, and all Laurel's negative resolutions died a premature death. Oh, hell, she thought, and I meant to be so chic and immaculate!

She let him in and he looked down at her feet. 'Love your bare toes, Laurie,' he said.

She promptly hid one foot behind the other, but she couldn't hide them both. 'You're almost an hour early.'

'Fifty minutes. I couldn't stay away. I missed you too much.'

Laurel didn't know what to say, but she knew what she felt. Whether it was genuine or not, she was very susceptible to his charm. She was also susceptible to his looks. For a man who wasn't conventionally handsome, he was devastatingly attractive in a dark suit, white shirt and tie. 'Very pukka,' she observed.

'I thought you might find me less alarming if I looked like an Englishman. I hope you appreciate the sacrifice.'

'Englishmen doesn't usually carry around roses. Are they for me?'

'Sorry, I forgot about them. It's the mind-blowing effect you have on me.' Connor looked around the kitchen-cum-living-room, which was still full of his previous roses, and went on, 'I'm glad you didn't throw them all away.'

Laurel carried the fresh bunch over to the sink, where she stood them in a bowl of water so they could have a good drink before she arranged them. 'I'm trying not to take out my aggression on poor helpless things that can't fight back.'

'Does that include me?' he asked, coming over to her.

She laughed, then touched one of the roses. 'Why always yellow?'

Connor touched her fair hair, and it was all Laurel could do to stop herself turning her face to nuzzle his hand. 'You're my golden girl, didn't you know? Yellow is the closest I can get to it in roses, and that's not so far off. You were wearing yellow the first time I saw you, and it just happened to be a yellow rose in the bowl at that motorway restaurant. I'm sentimental, I suppose. Would you like a different colour?'

Laurel only believed the half of what he said, but she shook her head. 'No, I like the yellow. I've got used to them.'

'Are you sentimental, too, or getting used to me, or both?' he asked softly.

'You ask a lot of questions,' she replied, moving away from his disturbing presence and going into the bedroom in search of her slippers. She sat down on the bed to put them on and found him sitting beside her. 'Connor, you're behaving as if you've known me for years,' she complained, exasperated.

'I'm trying to catch up on all the years we've missed, and I may only have one evening.' He was looking around the room and he added, 'Besides, I'm scared to stay in one place too long in case I get painted white.'

Laurel knew what he meant. In the purge that had followed Alan's defection, she'd thrown out the posters, prints, bean-bags, fluffy rugs—every bit of clutter that had given the flat colour and personality. Then she'd painted all the walls and paintwork white. Only then had she been able to go on living there.

For the first time she felt defensive about the purity and starkness her soul had demanded, and she flushed slightly. She didn't lie about it, though. 'It was a ritual cleansing. I was clearing a man out of my life.'

Connor's eyes settled on her thoughtfully. 'You did a thorough job on the flat. How about yourself?'

'Very thorough. I don't clutter up my life with anything any more, including men.'

'That doesn't sound much like a cure to me.'

Laurel smiled, stood up and moved away from him again. 'That's because you're a man. My aims are opposed to yours, so naturally mine must be suspect. Want to give up and go home?'

'I never give up,' Connor told her, but he was still looking at her in that thoughtful way she didn't quite like.

'In that case, if you put yourself on the other side of the bedroom door and shut it, I'll get ready. It should be an interesting evening. Make yourself some coffee. I won't be long.'

'I've heard that before,' Connor replied, but he went out. He didn't make coffee, or sit on the couch in the living-area of the kitchen and read the newspapers and magazines stacked neatly on a coffee-table in front of it. He leaned against a kitchen counter, staring at the closed bedroom door, frowning deeply.

It was dawning on him that the more he found out about Laurel, the less he knew. It wasn't a situation he liked, any more than he liked that door closed between them. After fifteen minutes he knocked on it. 'I'm lonely out here. Do you need any help? I'm very good with zips.'

'If you can pull them up as well as down, you can come in,' Laurel invited, leaning towards the dressing-table mirror as she fixed ear-rings with a little pearl drop into her ears.

She straightened as he came in. She was wearing a thigh-length smoky blue and grey chiffon frock with a high neck and long sleeves, and the appreciation she saw in his eyes told her she'd made the right choice. She turned her back to him and lifted her hair aside to reveal the last few inches of zip that needed closing.

She felt his hands touch the nape of her neck, and it was all she could do not to quiver as the sensation was transmitted all over her body.

'I've never known a woman get ready so fast,' he said. 'It's usually at least an hour among the pots of paint.'

Laurel turned back to him and tilted up her face to his. 'Do I need more paint?'

Connor looked down at her. Her cheeks were faintly flushed and glowing, her eyes looked a softer blue than he remembered, and her pink lips—including the vulnerably bitten lower one—were softly parted. She looked intoxicatingly natural and kissable, and he said abruptly, 'No, you don't.'

Something about his manner failed to reassure her, and she raised her hands to lift her hair to the top of her head. She turned her face this way and that so he could study her profile and the curve of her beautiful neck. 'What do you think, up or down? I couldn't make up my mind.'

It was all too much for Connor and he told her bluntly, 'Love you flirting with me, Laurie, but unless you want me to follow through, pack it up.'

Laurel froze. 'I am not flirting with you.'

'Yes, you are. It's great, but I'm not going in any sin-bin when I've been deliberately turned on. You know what a low flashpoint I have with you. What do you want, me on my best behaviour or following my natural instincts?'

Laurel released her hair and stepped back as though she'd been stung. For a few seconds his touch and his closeness had beguiled her into behaving as naturally with him as he did with her, and this was the result. She could only blame herself, and that made her squirm with embarrassment.

She tried to cover it with briskness. 'I want you on your best behaviour and I can guarantee I'll be on mine. Right, I'm ready.'

Connor picked up the coat she had put on the bed and held it out for her. 'Laurie,' he said uneasily, 'I was only trying to point out you can't expect me to stick to the rules if you break them yourself. That's fair enough, isn't it?'

'Absolutely,' she agreed, and smiled at him, but distantly—and that was how she remained for the rest of the evening.

At war with herself, she punished him. She knew she was doing it, but she couldn't help herself. She was polite, appreciative and attentive—and as remote as the moon.

The pub was all he'd said it would be. Over a delicious meal which she was entirely unconscious of eating they talked about his work and hers, discussed books, the theatre and films, without any real communication at all. They might have been two strangers on a blind date that had gone disastrously wrong.

Laurel parried personal questions with professional expertise and asked none in return. She erected a barrier which Connor, for all his skill, couldn't break down. Eventually he'd had enough and said, 'It was a tactical error when I kissed you at my place, and another when I didn't kiss you at yours. Do you mind telling me why?'

'Maybe I just don't like tactics,' Laurel murmured, sipping her wine. 'They make me feel too much like a target.'

In desperation he tried, 'Love you when I don't understand you, Laurie.'

She smiled. 'You're very free with your love, Connor.'

'And you're not?'

'I don't believe in it.'

Connor gave up and took her home. Outside her door she said politely, 'Thank you for a lovely evening.'

'It was terrible. If it was my fault, I'm sorry. If it was yours, phone me.' He sounded justifiably bitter and he left her standing there, just as she deserved, but not as she'd expected.

No, she'd been waiting for an explosion of temper, but he was obviously more disgusted than angry. Laurel's fingers trembled slightly as she turned the key in the lock and let herself into the flat. She would much rather he'd been angry. Nobody stayed angry forever.

Disgust was different. It lingered. Look how long she'd stayed disgusted with Alan, and how it had warped her so that she'd been incapable of a real relationship ever since. She hated the idea of Connor thinking of her with disgust.

And yet he'd said, '. . . phone me.'

She wouldn't, of course. For one thing, she wouldn't know what the devil to say. For another, she'd driven him away, although not in the way she'd planned. Still, how was she to know that under the intoxication of his presence there would be a magical moment when she hadn't cared about the past or the future?

Without realising it, she had come out of her shell. Without knowing it, he'd driven her straight back in. It was comic, really, and she'd appreciate the joke when she stopped feeling so wretched.

The trouble was that, as Laurel prepared for bed, her wretchedness increased. The flat was no longer so pleasingly sterile. Connor's vital presence seemed trapped there, haunting her at every turn. If he'd come back she would have clung to him, only he didn't come back.

Tonight she hated him for not coming back. Tomorrow she would probably be grateful. Laurel sighed. She was still at war with herself, still didn't know what she really wanted. She was clinging to her shell and reaching out for Connor, and she couldn't have both.

Or could she?

Laurel stood stock still as she considered the possibility of sharing her London life with Connor, and keeping her Hampshire life totally secret from him. Would it be possible? Why not? Alan had managed to have his cake and eat it. Connor probably did the same. Why should it be different for a woman? It wasn't as if there would be anything shoddy about it. There was no other man involved.

The more she thought about it, the more Laurel realised it could be managed without affecting her highest priority of all—Lianne. She would be offering

Connor a bachelor's dream, an affair without commitment. And when it was over she could slip away into Hampshire without any of the dreadful knots to untie that had followed her broken engagement to Alan.

Without commitment there was no bond to be shattered, no accusations, no regrets. She would remain what she'd come to prize so highly, a free woman, answerable to no one, ready to cut loose if she found herself betrayed.

Laurel went to her dressing-table and took the framed photographs of Lianne out of the bottom drawer. She'd hidden them from Connor because there had been absolutely no reason why she should explain her past to him. There had been no need, not for one date, and now she blessed her foresight.

She went around the flat putting the photographs back in their proper places, and then she went to bed. Her dithering over, she slept more soundly than she had in a long time.

It was a false peace. When she awoke, her puritan streak had re-established itself and the affair she'd plotted so cold-bloodedly the night before seemed like a fantasy nightmare—or an unachievable dream. She got out of bed cursing Connor and pining for him. She was dithering again, and quite the worst part of it was that, this time, she knew she was the one who'd treated him badly. She found she couldn't forgive herself for that.

CHAPTER SEVEN

LAUREL, mourning her loss of decisiveness and objectivity, busied herself around the flat for most of the morning. She couldn't seem to concentrate on the problem of Connor as a whole. Her mind could only latch on to one small part of it—how unfair she'd been to him last night.

She desperately needed to say she was sorry. Several times she picked up the phone, only to drop it back in its cradle when she couldn't think of a thing to say. Her longing for him was as inarticulate as it was deep. Could this really be her . . . the girl who made her living out of words?

Laurel knew she was unsure of herself because she was unsure of him. She wasn't even certain he wanted her to phone him. How humiliating if he only wanted the satisfaction of hearing her apologise and the chance to hang up on her for a change . . .

She ran a distracted hand through her hair, too restless to mooch around the flat any longer. She decided to go jogging. She could get any shopping she needed on the way back, have lunch and see if she could think of some more interesting way to fill up the blank hours before work.

Blank hours, she thought; when had she ever suffered from them? Too much to do and not enough time to do it in was usually her problem. Connor had a lot to answer for. Or maybe she did, for having her chances and muffing them. How, oh, how could she re-establish contact if she couldn't even bring herself to talk to him?

Because she did have to re-establish contact somehow—and soon.

The problem caused Laurel to jog twice as far as usual without any solution presenting itself. She picked up a fresh loaf and some steak on the way back and, having slowed down, found she didn't want to go back to Hewitt House. She dawdled, feeling the cold strike her and the pervasive drizzle seep through her track-suit, and not caring too much.

She remembered Connor saying, 'You don't look after yourself very well, do you, Laurie?' and felt like banging her head against a brick wall. The man was always with her. She couldn't exorcise his image, and the awful thing was that she no longer wanted to.

Laurel passed a public telephone booth, paused then walked on. She still didn't know what to say and was beginning to think she never would. Then she passed a florist's and stopped dead. It was so easy for a man to say sorry. He just sent flowers. It was the subtlest form of sabotage, weakening resistance, putting romance where resentment had been.

Why couldn't she do the same?

Don't think, she told herself. Don't reason, just do it.

She walked into the shop and briskly ordered a yellow rose to be sent to Connor Dyson at the Mayfair offices of Dyson Enterprises (UK) Ltd. 'No message,' she said, paid, and walked out. If Connor didn't know who was sending him a yellow rose, and why, there really wasn't anything worth re-establishing.

Outside the shop her resolution faltered, and she felt the most colossal fool. Connor would very likely think she was crazy. She ran the rest of the way home, as embarrassed as any sixteen-year-old who had lost her courage after manoeuvring a contact with a man.

Laurel prepared an early lunch, more for something to do than because she was hungry, and forced herself to concentrate on reading the newspapers while she ate. Connor mustn't be allowed to affect her work, and she couldn't turn up for her shift without knowing what had been going on in the world during the past twenty-four hours.

Most of the papers carried pictures of the charity match, featuring the bustier of the Celebrity players. Curiously enough, there was one shot with her and Lady Letitia in the background. She frowned over it, wondering whether Connor had been honest about his reason for going to the match, or whether he'd successfully bluffed his way out of a difficult situation.

Who dares wins, Laurel reminded herself. And Connor hadn't got where he was in the property world without one hell of a nerve. It would be unrealistic to suppose he didn't apply the same tactics to his private life.

Tactics. She hated the word. It had nothing to do with romance and, for all his charm, she'd always been aware Connor had the overlying assurance of a man who knew exactly what he was doing—and why.

Which was more than she did.

The more Laurel looked at the picture, the more she wondered whether he'd really known she'd be there. True, he'd zeroed in on her at the party, but perhaps he could afford to shelve Lady Letitia temporarily because he had her precisely where he wanted her. Perhaps the same fate lay in store for herself.

Connor must have a very ruthless streak to be as eligible as he was and still reach the age of thirty-five without getting seriously involved with any woman. All of which made him as much of a challenge as he apparently found her. It would be quite something to take him on at his own game and beat him.

Laurel, despairing of herself, discovered she didn't want to beat him but only to get to know him. She wouldn't be a willing victim, but she would risk herself a little if he responded to the yellow rose in a romantic way. She wouldn't be able to help herself, and the uneasy thought crossed her mind that he wasn't so very far from having her where he wanted her.

The phone rang and Laurel jumped out of her skin, a sign of how strung up her nerves were. With a skipping heart she answered, and felt a curious mixture of relief and regret when she heard Shirley say, 'Ah, got you at last! Where were you last night? Out with Connor Dyson? I'm bursting to know what's going on between you two.'

'What makes you think anything's going on?' Laurel bluffed.

'Come off it, darling, this is the girl Connor nearly mowed down to get to you—and it's the first time in years I've seen you letting a man get away with acting as if he owns you. Does he?'

'No.'

'Do you wish he did?'

'Of course I don't.'

'You're not convincing me,' Shirley told her breezily. 'Since when did you get yourself cornered unless you wanted to? I'm just ringing to say I'm happy for you, and to welcome you back to the land of the living. It isn't safe and it often hurts, but it beats being dead. If I'd known you'd been waiting all this time for a good-looking millionaire, I wouldn't have worried about you half so much.'

'Shirley, you're jumping to conclusions . . .'

'Not me! I'm a journalist, too, remember. I believe what I see with my own eyes and precious little else. Don't get in a tizz, I'm not going to spoil anything by prying. You know where I am if you want to talk. Cheers!'

The line went dead and Laurel went thoughtfully back to her newspapers. If the feeling between herself and Connor was so obvious that an onlooker like Shirley could believe in it, why couldn't she believe in it herself?

The question stayed with her, ruining her concentration, making her more restless than ever. The flat seemed claustrophobic, especially with Connor's roses all around her. A lot of them were wilting, but she couldn't bring herself to throw them away. She found herself wondering whether he'd be embarrassed by the rose she'd sent him. Well, he couldn't be more embarrassed than she was. She wished like mad she'd never sent it. How could she have broken her own golden rule: always have your second thoughts first?

She'd run the whole gamut of emotions since meeting Connor, but she didn't think any of them were more uncomfortable than being stuck with an impulse she bitterly regretted. Suddenly Laurel knew she had to get out of the flat. She needed fresh air, space, more room to panic in.

Hours too soon she got ready for work, wearing her silver-grey raincoat over a grey jersey dress. She had the romantic impulse to wear yellow accessories, but she squashed it firmly and settled for pink. She'd gone over the top once today, she wasn't going to do it twice.

She drove first to Hyde Park, which was the biggest space she could think of, then she changed her mind and headed for Green Park, just a stone's throw from Connor's Mayfair house. Once she'd parked, she looked for a phone booth. If she'd judged Connor's romantic streak wrongly and made a fool of herself, she wanted to know. She was sick to death of dithering.

She was very fair. She used his office number so his secretary could give her the brush off, if that was what he wanted, but as soon as she said her name she was put through. Her heart turned over as she heard his voice, warm and intimate, say, 'Love your yellow rose, Laurie.'

Anxiety and tension drained out of her. Trust Connor to come straight to the point, she thought, loving him, too. 'It seemed the least I could do after being such a bitch,' she told him.

'I never called you that.'

'No, it was your restraint that was so unnerving. Are you busy?'

'Not if there's a chance of seeing you,' he replied promptly. 'I know you're not at home. I've just phoned there.'

'I'm at Green Park. I wondered if you fancied a walk . . .'

Connor didn't hesitate or point out that it was raining. He just said, 'Meet you by the tube station in a few minutes,' and hung up. Either he did have a strong romantic streak or he knew how to play on hers, but Laurel wasn't bothered which right then. She just felt dizzy with anticipation.

In hardly any time at all she saw him come out of Stratton Street and cross Piccadilly, the collar of his suede jacket turned up against the cold, his thick brown hair beaded with fine rain. Her heart constricted with something very like pain. The day didn't seem meaningless any more.

Laurel moved forward to meet him and found herself not so much greeted as taken over. He kissed her cheek as though they'd been lovers for years and, such was his assurance, she almost felt that way herself. Then he took her umbrella and put an arm around her waist to hug her against his side so they could both get under it.

As they walked towards the park entrance he said, 'I'm thirty-five years old and I thought I knew it all—but I've never been sent a rose by a beautiful woman and taken for a walk in the park. What happens if I'm led into the bushes? Do I scream?'

Laurel began to laugh so helplessly that she relaxed against him and her head came to rest against his shoulder. Her hand came up to clutch his lapel as she steadied herself, and she didn't let go. It was nice, holding on to Connor.

Connor took instant advantage, as he always did, and bent to kiss her hair. 'Love you when you laugh, Laurie. You don't laugh enough. How much time have we got to work on that?'

'My shift starts at six.'

He grimaced. 'No time to waste, then, is there? We'd be a lot cosier in my flat.'

'I want to walk. I always do when I need to think or—or sort myself out. Plenty of space helps somehow, I suppose because I'm a country girl. Am I making any sense?'

'You don't have to make sense, Laurie. You just have to be with me.'

What a lovely thing to say . . . She turned her face towards his shoulder to hide a sudden rush of emotion. How could she fight a man who sabotaged her at every turn? Either he was very clever or very genuine. Laurel felt a touch of gloom as she pondered which.

Connor gave her a warning squeeze. 'When you go quiet, I start worrying. It means you're thinking, and whenever you start thinking I end up in the dog-house. Stick with your impulses, Laurie. They're crazy, and I love you to death for them.'

'Oh.' There she was, sabotaged again. She grumbled half-heartedly, 'You were supposed to call me Laurel like everybody else, and you never do.'

'Yes, well, I thought you might get to like Laurie if you heard it enough. I need a special name for you. It makes you seem more mine.'

He was going much too fast for her, as usual, and she looked up at him indignantly, but he was smiling at her in such a way, her protests died. She found herself explaining, 'I was brainwashed at a very early age. My mother always had a fit if anybody shortened my name, and I suppose I've just followed suit.'

'That's all right, then,' Connor replied breezily. 'She can have a fit at me any time and I won't take a blind bit of notice, so long as you're happy.'

'You're quite safe,' Laurel told him drily. 'She lives in Geneva.'

'Who do you visit in Hampshire, then?'

I walked right into that one, Laurel thought, and replied briefly, 'My aunt and uncle.'

Connor's lips touched her hair again, so lightly and yet so very possessively. 'Tell me about your family,' he said softly. 'There are all those blank years still waiting to be filled in.'

'There's not a lot to tell. As a family, we're civilised rather than close. My father has his own advertising agency and my mother was a model. They fought like mad and never knew what to do about me. They solved the problem as soon as I was old enough by sending me to boarding-school.' Laurel paused and glanced at him. 'You really want to hear all this? It's a very boring story.'

'You could never bore me, Laurie.'

She smiled. 'I hope I don't have to remind you of that.' Then she realised she was talking as if they had a future together and she went on hastily, 'I loved school. It was the holidays I hated, especially when my parents began leading separate lives under the same roof. It was a relief when they split up.'

'What happened to you?' Connor asked.

'I more or less fell on my feet. My father went to Canada to set up an advertising agency there and my mother married a Swiss banker. Aunt Sue—her older sister—and Uncle John were paid to look after me during the holidays. They were very good to me, and still are.'

Laurel broke off, thought, and added, 'Remarkably good considering they didn't have children of their own and never missed them because they're a complete unit by themselves. They're the ones I turn to if—if I'm in a pickle. I get scolded, but I also get helped. I suppose that's what a real family is all about.'

'It is,' Connor replied. 'I'm lucky, I've got one. Do you ever see your parents?'

He felt her shrug as she replied, 'I last saw my father two years ago when he was in London to link up his agency with one here. He's in love with success, and he's very successful so he's happy. I see my mother two or three times a year when she comes over for Ascot or the fashion shows. She's in love with herself, her husband spoils her, so she's happy, too.'

'What about you?'

'I'm in love with independence. I've got it, so I'm not complaining,' Laurel replied brightly. 'One thing about having cheque-book parents is that it's smashing to be able to say, "No, thanks, I can sign my own cheques now".'

Connor was quiet for so long that she said glumly, 'I told you it was a boring story.'

'I wouldn't have missed it for the world. At least I know now why you're not very good at relationships.'

Laurel almost grimaced as she thought of all the crucial things she'd left out. Falling for Alan had released all the love she'd had pent up inside her. She'd squandered it recklessly on him, believing herself loved and wanted at last. She'd never thought to protect herself.

Now she was so good at it, she couldn't stop, even when she wanted to, and her fierce protective urge extended to Lianne as well. Connor didn't know anything about that and she'd no intention of telling him, not unless the miracle happened and she found she could trust him.

For the moment she was only prepared to risk that part of her existence she could retreat from, if necessary. She wasn't going to let him get anywhere near the inner core. True, when he was close like this and so, so charming she was almost seduced into trusting this feeling between them—but almost wasn't good enough.

Connor said, 'Laurie, you're making me nervous. You've gone quiet again.'

She smiled. 'I was just thinking that when a man accuses a woman of not being very good at relationships, he's miffed because she prefers to manage her own life.'

'Ah.' He sounded as though he'd hit a snag. 'Are you a raving feminist?'

'I don't need a man to give me a reason for living, if that's what you mean.' But, even as she said it, Laurel had her doubts. Her uncertainty made her change the subject. 'What about your family? I gather you're close?'

'Very. I have two sisters with families of their own, which gives me four nephews and one niece. Mum and Dad are still happily together in Melbourne. They're coming over for Christmas. Would you like to meet them?'

'No!'

She was so unflatteringly definite that he frowned. 'Thanks. I'm very choosy who I ask to meet my parents.'

Laurel's cold cheeks warmed with embarrassment. 'I'm sorry, I never meant to be so rude. It's just that I have a horror of . . .' She hesitated.

'Getting involved,' Connor said for her. 'I got that message from the beginning. What you can't seem to get through that lovely head of yours is that we *are* involved, right up to our ears. I don't know about you, but I'm sinking.'

Her heart missed a beat, then raced to make up for it. She wanted to hug him and say it was all right, she was sinking, too, but she couldn't. She could only make a joke of it. 'Anybody would sink in this rain. Let's get off the grass and on to the path.'

For a second she thought he was going to get wild at her, but he must have reconsidered because he only said, 'We've run out of grass, path and park. What now?'

'We cross The Mall to St James's and walk around

the lake.'

'It's a pond,' he scoffed, guiding her across the road.

'To an Aussie, maybe. To a native like me it's a lake. When you're a guest in a country, you have to be polite and indulge the natives.'

'Yes, ma'am.' Connor lost his truculence and grinned down at her. 'Are there any native rituals or dances I should know about?'

'We've given them up. Every time we dance it rains.'

Connor laughed, looked down into her upturned face and suddenly grew serious. He swung her around so that she felt herself held against his chest, and heard him say huskily, 'Laurie, love, I've just got to kiss you.'

She stood absolutely still, half expectant, half anxious, caught up in a moment of longing she was helpless to resist. Her lips were cold and the lower one hardly healed from yesterday's match, but he kissed them very gently. Laurel felt warmth stealing over her, and an irrepressible yearning for more.

If only this was all that mattered, she thought wistfully, this feeling of belonging, of rightness. He kissed her again and there was no mistaking the way their lips clung, demanding more.

Her eyes had closed and it was real struggle to open them when Connor raised his head and breathed against her hair, 'That's what I call being involved. What do you call it?'

Laurel drew away from him and started to walk on. She wanted to separate herself altogether while she sorted out her emotions, but he wouldn't let her. His arm stayed around her waist, keeping her very firmly against his side. He must know, clever Connor Dyson, that she couldn't think dispassionately when he was so close.

'Laurie?' he prompted.

She was becoming so fond of his pet name for her that she weakened further, and had to think hard for her reasons for resisting him. 'I told you, I haven't room for a man in my life. I'm flat out with my career and—and making my own way.'

'And I told you that if I couldn't make room for myself I'd leave you alone. Is that what you want?'

Laurel thought of the misery without him that morning, the healing touch of his lips, and whispered, 'No.'

His lips brushed her hair again in that lover-like way that drained her strength and resistance. 'Then where do we go from here?' he asked. 'Don't tell me anything flip like a walk around the pond to look at the ducks. I mean us. You and me.'

It sounded like an ultimatum and she wasn't ready for that. She thought of Lianne and all she had to protect—everything she felt she had to hide from him just to be safe—and her hand crept up to clutch at his lapel again in an unconscious appeal for understanding.

'I have so little time to spare. I can't afford to let my career slip and I *have* to be independent. It's the way I am. Frankly, considering the way you are, I think I'd drive you up the wall.'

'What if I was willing to risk it?' Connor asked. 'Would you be?'

Laurel sighed. 'You're way ahead of me, as usual. I've had one commitment in my life, I'm not ready for another. I don't know if I ever will be. The way we are at the moment suits me—friends getting to know each other without any pressure. If that's not enough for you, we'd better finish whatever there is between us right now.'

Connor considered that for so long, she began to think that what had appeared possible to her that morning, when she'd been missing him so dreadfully, had always been hopeless. Had she really supposed she could offer such a negative situation to such a positive person like Connor and get away with it?

Her hopes, his silence, was the difference between dreams and reality. The two had never really matched up. She'd been a fool to suppose they ever might.

Connor said at last, 'What you're telling me is that your career comes first and I can have any time that's left over?'

'Apart from my trips home. That's a side of my life that has nothing to do with you. I'd feel—pressured if the two got mixed up.' What she really meant was that she couldn't be completely honest with him until she found out whether she could trust him. It was a bit like trying to dive in the pool while keeping one foot on the side, but it might just work out. If they cared about each other enough to make it.

Laurel glanced up and found him looking at her in that disconcertingly thoughtful way of his that made her feel he was reading between the lines and not making such sense of it. She couldn't blame him, and yet she wanted so much not to lose him.

'You're not offering much, are you, Laurie?' he asked. When she didn't answer, he came to a decision. 'All right, whatever you're offering, I'm taking. Consider us friends.'

She smiled, suddenly, brilliantly. Maybe, just maybe, Connor really was different from the picture painted of him in the gossip columns. Relief from anxiety made her light-headed and her smile became a chuckle. 'Good, because we're already friends. It's not every man I let carry my umbrella, you know.'

Connor stopped and swung her towards him again. 'It's not every man you let kiss you, either, is it?'

Her smile faded and she shook her head.

'That's what I thought,' Connor said with satisfaction. 'Like it or not, Laurie, we're more than friends. I'll make do with that . . . for the time being.'

Laurel, looking uncertainly at his confident expression, had the uneasy feeling she wasn't as much in control of the situation as it appeared. Connor had the disconcerting habit of seeming agreeable, then twisting everything his way and taking over.

No, her position wasn't so strong at all. It was extremely vulnerable. She felt the familiar flutterings of panic, made all the worse because the time to pull back had already passed. What happened next didn't depend on her so much as on Connor, and she wondered exactly who had manoeuvred whom into this situation.

Connor's arm tightened around her in a warning squeeze. 'You're thinking again and you know it's not allowed. I'm going to take you home, warm you up and fuss you so much, you'll be very sorry you're working tonight. And no arguments,' he added as she opened her mouth to protest.

'Bossy Aussie,' Laurel muttered darkly.

'Bolshie pommy sheila,' Connor replied promptly. 'If we're going to play name games, I'd better warn you mine get very dirty. You'd lose.'

'Then I won't play. I'm not a good loser.'

'Neither am I.' He replied so positively that she knew he was talking about a lot more than games. It was what she needed. Unwittingly, he'd made her feel competitive again. 'What are you grinning at?' he asked suspiciously.

She wrinkled her nose at him. 'I'm thinking how sweet you look carrying my umbrella.'

Connor swore at her and she laughed. For the first time in years she felt deliriously happy and she didn't spoil the moment by questioning it.

Back to the land of the living, Shirley had called it. Re-crossing the Mall with Connor and hurrying back through Green Park to beat the rapidly falling darkness of the early winter night, Laurel felt one hundred per cent alive. And she liked it. She liked it very much indeed.

CHAPTER EIGHT

WHEN they came out of Green Park in the rain-shrouded twilight the bustling world closed in on them and, like a chameleon, Laurel adjusted automatically to new surroundings. She tried to take his arm from around her waist, but he resisted. She stopped walking and looked up at him indignantly.

The commuter rush to the tube station was well under way and people milled around them like ants confused at finding an unexpected obstacle in their way. Connor didn't care. He just grinned down at her and said, 'I have to hang on to you to get us both under the umbrella.'

'That's not true, and we can't walk through Mayfair all wrapped round each other,' Laurel protested. 'Somebody might see us.'

His grey eyes teased hers. 'Most girls like to be seen with me.'

She looked away. She couldn't win an argument looking into Connor's eyes. 'I'm not most girls.'

'No, you're pretty special—and woolly-headed with it. Gossip column spies hang out in night-clubs, not freezing wet streets. Relax, there isn't a thing to worry about.'

Worrying, though, was a habit Laurel couldn't give up easily. 'Connor . . . please.'

'The things I do for a "please",' he sighed. He

115

released her waist but, as they walked on, his hand, big, warm and strong, closed over hers. 'Stick close and not even Sherlock Holmes will detect I've got you in my evil grip. Just be careful not to trip over your bustle.'

Laurel smiled. 'I'm not old-fashioned, I'm cautious.'

'You're also cold.' Connor thrust their clasped hands into the pocket of his sheepskin jacket. 'That better?'

'Mmm.' Connor in this mood was like a big cuddly bear, cosy and hard to resist. Not that she was resisting. 'What are you smiling about now?' she asked.

'We've just bickered without ending up at each other's throats. Maybe we should make it champagne instead of coffee.' He looked down at her. 'You realise what this means? We're both on the same side of the fence at last.'

'Unless we're sitting on it, waiting to see which one falls off first.'

'You fall, I'll catch. It'll be one way of getting my arms around you,' Connor replied easily.

When they went into his house the receptionist greeted him with a big smile and handed him a package. 'The photographs you wanted in a hurry,' she explained.

'Thanks, Sara. I'm not available if anybody calls.' He took Laurel along the passage, and when he ushered her into the lift his arms went around her and he pulled her against him. 'There's not room for the two of us otherwise,' he explained blandly.

He was fibbing again, but Laurel didn't protest. It was too nice being in his arms, and there was a limit to what he could get up to in such a confined space. When they got to the top he pressed the 'down' button and they zoomed down and up again.

'You're a big kid,' Laurel protested, laughing and pulling open the cage door when they got to the top. She opened the other door and they both more or less fell out into the passage.

Connor grinned. 'Some chances are too good to be missed, and I have to be on my best behaviour now, haven't I?'

'Yes.'

'You're a hard woman, Laurie,' he sighed, letting them into his flat, taking her raincoat and hanging it up.

The flat was beautifully warm, but in the living-room he switched on the elegant electric reproduction of a nineteenth-century fire. The coals and bars glowed rosily and he explained, 'The central heating's efficient, but I like heat I can see.'

So did Laurel, but he was taking her hand and leading her, not towards the kitchen as she supposed, but to another door. 'The second bedroom,' he went on, leading her through it and opening another door to show her the bathroom en suite. 'Yours whenever you want to stop over—with no strings attached.'

He whisked her back into the living-room, along the length of it and through another door. The first bedroom had been blue and gold. This one was scarlet and white with a graceful, giltwood four-poster bed. 'The master bedroom,' Connor told her. 'Also yours whenever you stop over—but with very definite strings attached.'

'Connor . . .' Laurel began to protest, but he silenced her by kissing her nose.

'I'm not rushing you, I'm just showing you the options. Look around. If there's anything you don't like, tell me and I'll get it fixed. I'll get on with the coffee.'

Laurel did look around, but more to get herself together than anything. There was such a vicarious thrill in being hunted so blatantly by a man like Connor, she needed to stop floating, get her feet back firmly on the ground. He was an opportunist. Too much weakness and she wouldn't be looking at that elegant four-poster, she'd be in it.

She opened a door she took to be the bathroom and found herself in a walk-in wardrobe amid Connor's suits and shoes. It was all so personal, she backed out hastily, feeling, in spite of his invitation, as though she were prying. The next door she opened revealed a bathroom that was definitely in the twentieth century.

It was completely mirrored, and everywhere she looked a glowing woman looked back. Connor had woken her up, switched her on, and it showed. He must know it, and it explained why he was so darned confident.

Laurel brushed her windswept hair and went back into the living-room. It seemed empty without Connor and she walked on to the kitchen, leaning against the doorway. He'd set out the tray and was waiting for the percolator to start bubbling. 'What do you think?' he asked.

'It's a lovely flat. It would be a crime to alter

anything.'

His grey eyes swept over her, taking their time. 'You suit the place better than I do. For me, it's just a place to rest my head. I'm turning Cherisham into my real home. I'll take you down there as soon as I can fix it, see what you think.'

'There won't be any time for that,' Laurel replied, knowing what a traitor she'd feel, going into Hampshire without visiting Lianne. She also felt a prickle of warning, remembering what the gossip item had said about him, Lady Letitia and the manor. 'Buying the estate wasn't just a bit of property speculation, then?'

'No. I've got this flat, one in New York and a place in Melbourne, but now I'm ready to move the company into Europe as well, England makes the best base for it all. Cherisham is the first real home I've had in years.'

The percolator began to bubble and the delicious smell of coffee filled the kitchen. 'Smells good,' Laurel said, not wanting to think what a hazard having Connor living virtually on her doorstep could become.

'You're changing the subject,' Connor said.

'Well, it's nothing to do with me, is it?' she replied. She hurried on before he could answer, 'I never did find out why you involved yourself in buying up the leases on Hewitt House and the other blocks.'

'I had contracts to sign with builders, architects and designers, and it was all taking too long. Besides, I've been a tenant myself and I thought that if there were any gripes, I should be the one to hear them.'

Laurel, trying to push Cherisham and Lady Letitia out of her mind, smiled. 'And you had me down as one of the gripers?'

Connor poured the coffee and smiled back. 'I still have—sometimes. Are you hungry?'

Laurel shook her head and moved out of the way as he carried the tray into the living-room. She sat at the end of the couch closest to the fire and he sat on the couch opposite, which surprised her. Had he remembered he wasn't supposed to go too fast for her? Or was he pursuing a deliberate policy of blow hot, blow cold to keep her intrigued? She couldn't tell. She could only remind herself she was dealing with a very clever man.

They sipped their coffee. She was conscious of how closely he was watching her, then he said abruptly, 'You said once that you fix up your shifts on a Thursday. Leave Friday night free. We'll go out to dinner.'

Friday. Today was only Monday. So he was deliberately slowing the pace to make her unsure of herself. It might have been what she'd said she'd wanted, but she was piqued all the same. 'I'm not sure I can do that. It depends if I can get a day shift to compensate.'

'I hate you working all hours for peanuts,' he said, and she thought what he really hated was her not falling in with his plans immediately. His women—all of them!—must have spoilt him terribly.

'What's peanuts to you is a high income to me, and most other people,' she retorted. 'What's special about Friday, anyway?'

'I'm flying to New York tomorrow and I won't be back until Friday. I don't suppose there's any chance of you coming with me?'

Laurel was so taken aback, she could only shake her head. He spoke of New York as if it were just down the road on the bus, and as if her job was something she could play ducks and drakes with. She wondered if he ever really to listened to anything she said.

'Promise me Friday evening, then,' he went on.

Laurel promised. His attitude might irritate her, but that didn't stop her heart singing because he wanted to see her again as soon as possible. So much, she thought wryly, for getting her feet back firmly on the ground.

She was rewarded with a smile that had her floating again, then Connor was saying, 'I'll pick you up around eight, and I'll phone you every day.'

Laurel replied hastily, 'No, don't do that. It would seem——'

'We're involved, whether you like it or not,' he interrupted. 'I thought we'd got that straight.'

'Yes, but I might be sleeping or working. There's no telling with me.' What she was really afraid of was becoming dependent on hearing from him. She had to go on as though he were something extra grafted on to her life. She mustn't let him become an integral part of it.

Connor regarded her sombrely. 'Sometimes you act as if you've something to hide. You sure there's not another man in your life?'

'Absolutely.'

He looked unconvinced. 'When the English say "absolutely", it sounds so honest, but it's usually designed to cut off all discussion.'

'There's nothing to discuss. There's no other man.'

Laurel met his eyes steadily and he relaxed. He also came and sat next to her, reaching for the package he'd thrown on the table and opening it. As he took out the photographs he said, 'This morning I thought these might be all I'd ever have of you. I felt pretty bleak, I can tell you.'

He'd taken the photographs at the rugby match and they were all of her—clean, muddy, laughing, solemn. Some were full length, some close up, and they all bore out his story that he'd only gone to the match to watch her.

Connor was looking at the last photograph, taken just before the match ended. Her face was muddy, her hair tousled, and her lip was bleeding. 'I'm going to have to kiss you better again,' he murmured, and turned her face towards his.

They looked at each other and then their lips met and lingered. Laurel felt herself sinking into the bliss of the sweetest sensations, and her hand came up and touched his face. He kissed that too, then pulled her head down on his shoulder and held it there.

Laurel closed her eyes. She knew she was desired but, just for the moment, she felt loved and it was what she needed. She didn't expect Connor to share her content or for his restraint to last, and she was touched when he said, 'I think I'd better make some more coffee, or neither of us will be getting any work done tonight.'

'I thought you weren't busy,' Laurel replied, feeling a pang of guilt as he stood up and collected the coffee-cups.

'Nothing I can't catch up on. I haven't got any regrets. Have you?' When she shook her head he said, 'Fair enough,' and went into the kitchen.

Laurel wanted to follow him, but the kitchen now seemed dangerous territory with him in there. She suspected there was a limit to his restraint and that he was already close to it. Neither of them really wanted more coffee, it was just a way of keeping them apart, a situation that couldn't go on much longer. The feeling between them was too volatile, too intense.

She would have to come to a decision soon, or he would be making the decision for her. He was that sort of man.

Laurel wandered around the living-room, touching this ornament and that, a prey to the restlessness that had driven her to him in the first place. She had, in a funny sort of way, become accustomed to the hazard of falling in love with him, but liking him as well seemed infinitely more perilous.

Trying to stay immune was as hopeless as Canute trying to hold back the sea, and all the time the temptation to give up the struggle was increasing. There must be worse fates than sinking without trace into Connor's arms.

Lianne flashed across her mind, reminding her she was no longer a free agent to take risks and to hell with the consequences. She also, out of the blue, remembered what Lady Letitia had said when Connor picked her up after that sideline tackle: 'Trust it to be you, Connor. Always around when I need you.'

Laurel knew what she'd meant. Connor had the ability to make a woman feel safe, cared for, but it was an ability he obviously spread around a lot. And how many women's names did he shorten to make them more 'his'? Lady Letitia—Letty. Laurel—Laurie.

There could be dozens.

What made her think she was special, just because

he happened to say she was? Probably the special woman in his life at any given time was the one who was holding out, as she was. She felt her precarious happiness cracking under the weight of her doubts, and went into a different kind of panic. She wanted to believe in Connor, she really did.

He walked back into the room and her reeling world steadied. She looked at him—big, bronzed and with a face that was better than handsome because there was no other face she liked to look at as much. She felt a surge of fresh happiness, enough to drown her doubts, and she smiled radiantly at him.

Connor murmured, 'If a cup of coffee's worth a smile like that, I'll keep them coming.'

She laughed and stayed happy until it was time to go to work. Connor helped her into her coat and walked her to the lift. 'Don't come down with me,' she said. 'I'd rather say goodbye to you here.'

His arms came around her and he held her head against his shoulder again in a way she was getting used to. They stood like that for a few moments, neither moving, then Connor kissed her hair and told her, 'Until Friday.'

'Until Friday,' Laurel repeated.

'Miss me.'

It was a command and she didn't mind it. She nodded and stepped into the lift. He hadn't kissed her lips, but if he had she'd never have got to work. The feeling between them couldn't be played with, not any longer.

When she stepped out of the lift downstairs her decision was made, had really been made when those dynamic grey eyes of his had first locked on hers. Her fight had always been a losing one and she was past caring.

She just wanted to be happy with Connor. She was organised this time. If it didn't work out, she could cut loose with no harm done. Except, perhaps, to herself, and she was willing to risk that now. If, however, she found she could trust herself to him, then she would tell him about Lianne because she'd be able to trust her to him as well.

It conjured up a rosy picture and Laurel gave the receptionist a big smile as she passed her. She was still smiling as she went out of the front door and down the steps. Another girl passed her going up the steps as she paused to put up her umbrella. The girl had her head down, her umbrella up, and she clutched several couture shopping bags. It was very dark now, but the street lighting was good and Laurel got a swift glimpse of the girl's face.

It was Lady Letitia—Connor's Letty.

Laurel walked on, the silly smile trapped on her face as though that glimpse of Letty had turned it to stone. What was it Shirley had said? '. . . welcome back to the land of the living. It isn't safe and it often hurts, but it beats being dead.'

Laurel didn't know what it was like to be dead, but she did know what it was like to hurt. As she visualised Letty taking her place in Connor's flat, the hurt got worse and worse.

CHAPTER NINE

LAUREL went to work hoping she'd be sent out on a job challenging enough to take her mind off Connor. She was unlucky for the first couple of hours—routine work kept her at her desk. Thoughts of Connor remained very much with her, and her concentration was shot to pieces.

When she had to go down to the library for the file on a pop star who'd been arrested on a drugs charge, she also took out the file on Connor, needing some sort of contact with him, however tenuous. It was fairly thick and divided between his business and social activities. She concentrated on the personal stuff, and that was how she found out that eight years ago he'd been engaged to Australian model Holly Parkes, who'd later gone to Hollywood.

Laurel knew a little about Holly. She hadn't found stardom, but with two wealthy marriages behind her she often cropped up in the society pages of newspapers and magazines because she was rich, photogenic and played with the jet set.

Whatever had gone wrong with the engagement, it hadn't put Connor off women, Laurel mused. His name was linked with an endless stream of them after that. She sighed, closed the file and put it back. It hadn't helped. She still had to make up her own mind about him. She wanted him so much, but she didn't want to be just another name in the file. Nor would she share him.

By degrees she relaxed into a more rational frame of mind. Letty and Connor were friends, there was no earthly reason why she shouldn't visit him—and it had been during office hours.

Wanting to believe in him because she needed to, Laurel's hand strayed towards the telephone. If she phoned him and his replies were guarded, she'd know Letty was still with him—and yet it seemed horribly like spying. However she felt, she mustn't check up on him.

The time to start trusting him was now, not tomorrow or the day after. But it was hard, so very hard. Laurel was glad when she and a photographer were sent to cover a gun siege that had developed in North London after a quarrel between a man and his common-law wife. It wasn't half as exciting as it sounded, and by the time the police succeeded in persuading him to give himself up her shift was almost over.

She was in bed before two, but her brain was hyperactive and she slept fitfully. She was up again at seven, fighting the urge to phone Connor—not to find out what he had or hadn't been up to, but just to talk to him before he left for New York. Miss me, he'd said. As if she needed asking . . .

She was also missing Lianne. Torn between the two of them, she felt she was on a see-saw she couldn't balance properly. She decided to go home for the day. She checked the trains, then phoned Aunt Sue, telling her which one to meet. 'It will be less tiring than driving, and I'm working tonight,' she explained. 'Is Lianne up yet?'

'No, and I'm not going to wake her,' Aunt Sue replied in her forthright way. 'I believe in letting sleeping children lie. She'll be so excited when she knows you're coming, I won't be able to do anything with her.'

Laurel laughed, chatted a little longer, then got ready, wondering as she did so what could have possessed her when she'd told Connor not to phone her. It was much too late to worry about becoming dependent on hearing from him. She already was.

Her few hours with Lianne that day cheered her up and settled one of her worries. Falling for Connor hadn't robbed Lianne of any love, far from it. Love, she was discovering, only generated more love, until she felt she was overflowing with it.

On the way home again her mood was buoyant, hopeful. If the love was enduring and returned by Connor, then trust would surely follow. She'd have the two factors necessary to banish spectres like Letty—love and trust—and then her two separate lives would merge naturally.

It conjured up a rosy picture and she carried it with her through the days Connor was in New York, days kept deliberately busy to make them pass more quickly. She arrived at the flat from her day shift on Friday with plenty of time to spare, but she rushed around getting ready, thinking he might arrive early.

He did, and she loved him for it. If nothing else, they were on the same wavelength.

He was standing there on the doorstep with a large bunch of yellow roses and a gift-wrapped package, and Laurel wondered why she had ever thought he wasn't strictly handsome. She just couldn't seem to look at him enough, and from the look in his eyes she knew she'd been right to splurge on a new frock of fine, yellow wool that clung to her figure until it flared below a dropped waistline.

'Miss me?' Connor demanded without smiling.

Laurel nodded, and then he smiled. He also put a burly arm around her neck, pulled her head against his shoulder and kept her there. 'Miss me?' she asked, looking at his sun-tanned neck and wanting to kiss it.

'Too bloody right,' he murmured, bending his head to kiss her cheek, and then laying his face against hers in a way that seemed to say so much more than the most passionate embrace.

'Language,' she reproved, but mildly, thinking she wouldn't need much encouragement to stay like this forever. Connor wasn't in a hurry to move, either, and eventually she had to say, 'We're crushing the roses.'

'Do we care?'

'I do.' Reluctantly she drew back from him, took the roses and led him inside. He followed her right up to the sink and watched her stand them in a bowl of water. Then he gave her the package.

'You didn't have to bring me a present,' she said, unwrapping it.

'It's just a duty free. Couldn't waste my allowance, could I?'

It was a bottle of perfume but, more than that, it was the right one. 'Thank you,' Laurel said, then

raised her blue eyes to his. 'It says a lot about the kind
of life a man leads when he can identify what perfume
a woman wears.'

'Guilty,' Connor confessed, and grinned, 'but now
I've met you and I'm a reformed character.'

Laurel, as she fetched her coat, thought she had no
option but to take his word for it, at least for the time
being. Besides, she didn't want to worry about
anything this evening. She just wanted to be with
him. It was years since she'd been irresponsible
enough to let tomorrow take care of itself.

Connor noticed her changed attitude. He said, as he
settled her into his car, 'You seem so much more
relaxed tonight.'

'I mean to enjoy myself.'

'You and me both,' he replied, dropping a quick
kiss on her hair and going round to get into the
driver's seat.

Laurel listened to the deep growl of the powerful
engine and leaned back, turning her head against the
headrest to look at him. She felt spoilt and pampered,
and she loved it, but more than that she felt that if
they had just been holding hands and walking to the
fish and chip shop she'd have been just as content.

It was Connor she needed. She felt a qualm, but
pushed it aside. This was her night, *their* night, and if
anybody ruined it this time it wouldn't be her. He was
conscious of her regard, snatched a look at her and
asked, 'All right?'

'Fine. How about you? No jet lag?'

'Me, I'm fine. Couldn't be better. I feel like I've just
caught up with the part of me I left behind.'

Laurel swallowed. That was exactly what she felt, too, but she wasn't as uninhibited as him and couldn't say it. Instead she smiled. 'You never walk if you can run, do you, Connor?'

'Not if I can help it,' he replied cheerfully. 'How long have we got together? I mean, when are you working again over the weekend?'

'Day shifts Saturday and Sunday, then I'm off until Monday night.'

Connor grimaced. 'Then we'd better cram what we can into it. I'm flying back to New York on Monday night. I'll be gone about ten days.'

Laurel had trouble hiding her dismay. Ten days! The past four had seemed an eternity. But she knew she could get through them when he added, 'I have a couple of deals coming to the boil. I only flew back to see you.'

Now she not only felt spoilt and pampered, she felt cherished, too. But she couldn't help wondering whether the things he said that made her feel so good were genuine or part of a highly polished technique.

'I'm flattered,' she replied at last.

'You should be. It's years since I've let a woman get between me and business.'

That would have been Holly Parkes, his one-time fiancée, Laurel guessed. She waited for him to elaborate. He didn't, so she said slowly, 'I can't afford to let you get between me and my work, Connor.'

'You've made that clear enough, Laurie.'

'Yes, but is it a situation you accept?'

'Sure . . . until I can change it.'

He sounded so irrepressible, Laurel laughed and

surrendered again to the intoxication of just being with him. As they left the town behind and headed into Surrey, she asked, 'Are we going to the same pub?'

'No, a roadhouse. The tucker's great and the lighting's so discreet you need a guide dog to get around, but the real attraction is the dance-floor. It'll give me a legitimate reason for getting my arms around you.' Connor shot her a smiling glance. 'Scared?'

'I'll make sure my knees knock in time with the music so nobody notices,' Laurel promised.

He laughed and his hand came over and covered hers. The pressure was light, the contact brief, but it reinforced how much her body welcomed his touch. 'You're bad for my blood pressure,' he told her. 'Am I bad for yours?'

It was another of his leading questions, and she dodged it. 'When you drive with one hand on the wheel, yes.'

He laughed again, and after that they always seemed to be laughing. They dined on lobster thermidor and Connor talked about the business deals that were to take him back to the States on Monday. Laurel told him about some of the stories she'd covered that week, and when she fell silent he began to speak about Cherisham.

'You love the place, don't you?' Laurel asked.

'Well, I have a lot of places to live, but no proper home. As soon as I saw the manor I knew that was it. I bought it on the spot.'

'Do you always make up your mind that fast when

you want something?'

'Always,' he replied, and the way his grey eyes bored into hers made her flush slightly and reach for her champagne.

'I don't make snap decisions any more,' she replied. 'I always have my second thoughts first. At least, almost always,' she corrected hastily as she remembered the rose she'd sent him.

'Here's to almost always,' Connor said, raising his glass to her in a smiling toast. 'I love you best when you're impulsive.'

So their minds had both jumped to the same thing, Laurel thought. It was uncanny how often that happened. The waiter came to clear away their plates and Connor told him, 'Don't hurry with the next course. We're going to dance.'

He took her hand and led her on to the small dance-floor where couples shuffled slowly in the limited space. Laurel found she was holding her breath while she waited for his arms to come around her, her anticipation was so great. And when they did she felt as though Alan had never existed and this was what she'd been waiting for all her life.

Whatever her mental reservations—and she couldn't remember for the moment what they were—her body knew where it wanted to be. It gravitated towards his, exulting in the hardness that it met, soft curves lapping against muscles until the two seemed indivisible.

Laurel's head came to rest naturally against his shoulder and she closed her eyes, giving herself up to pleasurable physical sensations that seemed to make a nonsense of everything else.

'Laurie,' Connor breathed. 'Laurie . . .'

'Ssh,' she said, although she would have been incapable of explaining why. She just wanted to surrender to this blissful feeling of belonging without comment or question. If it was a gross indulgence, she didn't want to know about it now.

Connor must have understood because he didn't say any more. His arm just tightened around her waist and his hand came up to hold her head against his shoulder. From time to time he kissed her hair, and when he lowered his head further to kiss her ear she shuddered and pressed against him more closely still.

The madness lasted for the length of the dance, and when the music stopped and they had to move apart Laurel felt disorientated. In a better world, she thought, the music would never stop and problems would be kept permanently at bay.

As it was, couples were leaving the dance-floor and she was still standing there, feeling foolish as she tried to pull herself together. Connor was still there, too, of course, but he didn't seem to give a damn who might be watching, so closely was he looking at her.

She wouldn't meet his eyes, not so much afraid of what she might read in them as what he might read in hers. To cover her embarrassment she laughed and said, 'It's a long time since I've danced. I'd forgotten what it was like.'

She knew that if it had ever been like this she wouldn't have forgotten, but he didn't question her and silently she blessed him for that. She also liked the way his arm remained around her waist as he led her back to the table as though he, too, was finding it hard to get to grips with reality.

Neither of them said anything as the waiter served them with grape brulée and topped up their glasses, but as soon as he'd gone Connor asked, with such abruptness she suspected the question had been on his mind for a long time, 'Laurie, how long is it since you cleared that man out of your life—you know, when you turned the flat into a clinic?'

A clinic? That jolted. She forced herself to see the flat through his eyes and realised he wasn't far wrong. Her answer was equally abrupt. 'Four years.'

'*Four years*! You mean there hasn't been a man in your life for that long, a girl as lovely as you?'

'As an affair, it taught me there's a lot to be said for a career,' Laurel answered shortly, and began to eat. 'Mmm, it's delicious. Do try it, Connor. It's meant to be eaten immediately.'

He picked up his spoon, but said, 'You mean you don't want to talk about it?'

'There's not much to be said. We were engaged but he didn't love me quite as much as he loved himself. When he got a great career opportunity in the States I was left behind—and dumped. My own career had faltered, so I had to start again from scratch. I don't ever intend to make the same mistake twice.'

'We're talking about Curtis, aren't we?' Connor pressed.

'You are, I'm not interested.' Laurel sipped her champagne. She didn't want to think about Alan. It would spoil everything.

But Connor wasn't going to be put off. 'If it's a

touchy subject, you must still feel something for him.'

'Not anything nice. I ended up despising him, if you really must know, and believing there are things more worth bothering with than men.'

Connor took her hand and held it. 'You're bothering with me.'

'I'm reacting to you, and that's not the same.'

He turned her hand over and bent his head to kiss the palm, then his lips moved on to her wrist and lingered. 'Here's to reacting, Laurie,' he murmured.

The wildest sensations shot up her arm and suffused her entire body, and his teasing eyes told her that he knew it. Laurel swore and he laughed, then she was laughing with him and everything was giddy and irresponsible again, the way she needed it to be.

They danced together several times, and would have stayed until the place closed if Laurel hadn't made the mistake of yawning. Connor put her from him, studied her and said, 'I'm being selfish. You've been working all day and you're working again tomorrow. I'd better take you home.'

She protested, but he wouldn't listen. Was he caring and concerned, she found herself wondering as he settled her in the car and got in beside her, or clever and calculating?

Connor started the engine, then asked, 'Why are you looking at me like that?'

Laurel waited until he'd edged out of the car park and on to the road before answering evasively, 'I was wondering how you keep your sun-tan in this climate. Sun-bed?'

'No, it's ingrained, but the sun's always shining

somewhere. If you want some, say the word and we'll go chasing it. You'd make such a cute little surfy bunny.'

'Just like that!' she marvelled, trying not to visualise the surf—and him.

'Why not?'

'Connor, we're living in different worlds.'

'We don't have to.'

'Yes, we do,' Laurel replied, feeling that reality was creeping in with a vengeance now, and there wasn't anything she could do about it. 'I'm not one of your society girls. I care about my independence and my career.'

'Strewth, Laurie, I was hoping that after this evening all that would be open to negotiation.'

'Thanks, but I'm not a piece of property!'

'If you were, I'd have snapped you up on the spot,' Connor drawled, unabashed.

In spite of herself, Laurel found herself laughing. 'And I thought it was only my flat you were interested in.'

'No,' he contradicted her calmly, 'you always knew it was a hell of a lot more than that. We both did. So where have we got to and where are we heading?'

Laurel was silent for so long, he spelled it out for her. 'We need to be together. Every time we touch tells us that. We're neither kids nor fools, so we can't pretend it isn't happening. I'm not hanging back, so why are you?'

'I suppose I'm not ready for a take-over bid,' she managed at last, but when she looked at him she saw that, for once, he wasn't ready to smile.

Instead he asked, 'Whose sins am I paying for? Mine? Curtis's?'

Laurel swallowed, caught between the twin fears of losing him and committing herself. She said in a very small voice, 'I did warn you about rushing me, Connor . . .'

He glanced at her, and what he saw in her face made him let her off the hook. 'So you did. Sorry, it's just that I'm an impatient man. I warned you about that, too.'

Laurel didn't know what to say and, as the silence grew, she began to wonder if they were drifting apart again. With his uncanny ability to read her thoughts, his hand came over and covered hers briefly, reassuringly. 'It's all right, Laurie. You might be a slowcoach, but you're still my favourite girl.'

She relaxed, but she also raised her eyebrows and asked, 'Do the others know?'

'What others? There aren't any others,' he told her as he parked outside Hewitt House.

'Oh? And I'm supposed to take your word for that?'

She was smiling, but for the first time that night she saw him frown. 'Too right you are. I'm taking your word there's no other fellow in your life. We won't last five minutes otherwise.'

'Seems like it's my turn to say sorry,' she said, searching in her handbag for the key, then exclaiming, 'You've already got a key!'

'It's my building, remember,' he replied, as he ushered her inside, put an arm around her waist and began to walk with her to the stairs. 'It's all right, I haven't got one to your flat—unless you'd like to give me one.'

Laurel shook her head at him. 'I was thinking of giving you a cup of coffee.'

'Great. Whatever you're offering, I'm taking. That's something we've got settled.'

A little later she was wondering why the flat always seemed to shrink in size when Connor was inside it. Perhaps it was his way of making himself so much at home. He had his jacket off and his tie loosened before she had the percolator on, and now he was following her around, supposedly helping her, but getting in her way.

Every time she brushed against him, or their fingers touched, her nerves jumped until she said breathlessly, 'Connor, if you want coffee, go and sit down.'

'I don't want coffee, I want you.' His hand came up and with a gentle finger he traced the outline of her lips. 'I think you know how much.'

Laurel stood absolutely still, her whole body tuned to the provocative way his finger began to move back and forth along her lower lip, until she could bear the torment no longer and caught it between her teeth. She let it go, but the desire remained and she said huskily, 'You don't play fair, Connor.'

'I'm not playing. Are you?'

She looked up into his grey eyes. They seemed to be looking into her very soul, just as they had when she'd first met him. She hadn't been able to resist them then and she couldn't now. Getting to know Connor had made her weaker, not stronger.

It took all her will-power to lower her eyes while

she frantically tried to think, but she only found herself looking at his white shirt with the tie loosened and the top button undone, revealing his strong, suntanned throat. She yearned to press her lips against that bare skin and her breasts against that white shirt.

With a sigh that was really a surrender, she reached across and switched off the percolator. There seemed no better way of saying that no, she wasn't playing either.

Connnor didn't give her a chance to change her mind. He crushed her to him, one hand on her back, the other on her hips, pressing her against his hard body. Laurel gasped with sheer pleasure and then, to her horror, she began to tremble. It had been so long, she'd forgotten the moves and she felt awkward, unable to respond as she wanted to.

'Hey . . .' Connor murmured against her hair and his arms loosened, as though he understood. He began to stroke her hair, gently, persuasively, so that Laurel's eyes closed and she began to relax. His hands moved to her back, beginning an unhurried exploration that made her shiver again, but this time in the most delicious manner.

She began to respond, her hands sliding up his back and across his shoulders in a thrilling exploration of her own. She opened her eyes, saw his throat where the collar was open and pressed her lips against it. She felt a deep shudder run through him that might have been her own, so deeply did it thrill her. She reached up to thread her fingers through his hair and used it to pull his face down to hers.

Their lips met and fused with an ecstasy that seared

Laurel to the depths of her being. They broke apart and looked at each other, and then Connor was pressing kisses all over her face and she held her head back to expose her throat for more. She was awash with sensation, but it only built up the urgency for their lips to meet again . . . and again.

His hands were on the zip at the back of her dress and she began to unbutton his shirt. He shrugged out of it as she stepped out of her dress and kicked it away, and he pressed her against his chest again with only the fragile silk of her slip between them.

Connor kissed his way down her neck to her shoulders and slid the straps from them. The slip caught at her hips, but neither of them noticed because now her bare breasts were pressed against his naked chest and they both gasped.

He turned her slightly from him, lifting her face to kiss and then his hand moved down to her breast, grasping and massaging it and then playing with her nipple. Laurel's groan of pleasure was lost against his lips and, as she felt her legs go weak, Connor picked her up and carried her into the bedroom.

He kicked off his shoes, threw back the quilt, put her on the bed and stood looking down at her while he took off the rest of his clothes. The curtains hadn't been closed and a surprisingly bright moon bathed them both in a silvery glow. 'Do you know how lovely you are?' he asked as he lay beside her.

He didn't expect an answer, and Laurel was quite incapable of giving one because his mouth had fastened on to her breast and his tongue was flicking her nipple into a frenzy of desire. He moved to the other breast and the delicous torment began anew.

'Connor . . .' she breathed, but he took no notice, sliding the petticoat from her hips, and then her stockings and suspenders, and kissing his way over the warm flesh he exposed.

'Connor . . .' she breathed again, writhing with the most exquisitely unendurable ecstasy she had ever known, but now his own passion overwhelmed him and he entered her, thrusting hard and desperately in the need to quench his own fires. Laurel held him fiercely, pressing his hips against hers as they sought and found a final explosion of passion.

Connor kissed her with hot, spent, grateful lips and then he collapsed against her, moving down to rest his sweating face between her breasts. Laurel pulled the quilt over them and cuddled him to her while their breathing returned to normal.

It was a long time before Connor stirred, then he rolled off her and propped himself up on his elbow and looked down at her. 'I'm crazy about you, Laurie,' he said huskily. 'How do you feel about me?'

Even after everything that had happened, the word 'love' refused to come to her lips and she replied, 'I'm here, and I'm not a one-night stander.'

He frowned down at her, 'For pity's sake, Laurie, you can't still be cautious, not after the way we are together. We have to talk.'

Laurel pushed him over on his back, then propped herself over him, her breasts brushing against his chest. 'I don't want to talk tonight. Tomorrow will do. Go to sleep.' She kissed his eyes shut and then she studied him, and it almost hurt her how handsome he looked with his face relaxed and the moon turning the sun-bleached ends of his brown hair to silver.

She kissed his lips because she couldn't help herself, and then she kissed her way down to his chest, where she rested her head and settled herself for sleep.

'Laurie,' he asked softly, 'are you making love to me?'

'No, I'm going to sleep,' she mumbled.

'I think we might have a bit of a problem, love.' When she raised her head and looked at him questioningly, he added, 'I want you again.'

Laurel moved her hand down his body, found he wasn't kidding, and heard him say, 'I think it's found home at last and doesn't want to leave it.'

Connor claimed her with a slow and sensuous loving that was so different from the frantic passion of the first time that she was moved to tears. She felt as if he was using his body to tell her how much he cared for her, and she could only respond the same way, welcoming this way of expression that needed no impetuous and perhaps Judas words. There was no betrayal here, she knew, not tonight.

Tomorrow, she thought as she fell asleep in his arms, would be soon enough to discover what trust she could put into words . . .

CHAPTER TEN

THERE was precious little time for words or anything else when Laurel opened her eyes in the morning. For the first few seconds she was conscious only of Connor beside her and his arm lying heavily across her waist. She raised herself cautiously and looked at him.

He was still fast asleep, his hair tousled, his face so dear to her. Laurel kissed his cheek tenderly. He mumbled something and pulled her down against him, his other arm coming round her to cradle her to his chest. She smiled, nestled close and closed her eyes.

They opened again almost immediately, registering something she'd only been subconsciously aware of before. The room wasn't filled with the grey gloom of dawn, but the full brightness of wintry sunshine. She gasped, raised herself to look at the bedside clock and was out of Connor's arms and the bed in a trice.

She tripped over her dressing-gown, which had slipped from the top of the quilt to the floor some time during the night, picked it up and was throwing it on as she made for the door. Connor sat up and demanded, 'Where do you think you're going?'

'To work. I've only got fifty minutes and the traffic's bound to be hell. I forgot to set the alarm last night,' she replied hastily.

'Laurie, come here.' The quilt had slipped to his hips and he held out a hand to her peremptorily.

She looked at his naked torso and wavered. Half of her was frantic to get ready for work, the other half succumbing to his magnetism, and she would have gone to him if he hadn't continued, 'You don't have to work any more. I'll take care of you.'

That strengthened her, because it brought back forcefully how she'd made her career secondary to Alan, and lived to regret it bitterly. She forced a smile and said lightly, 'Thanks, but I'm the girl who prefers to be independent, remember?'

Laurel whisked herself out of the room and into the bathroom. She showered rapidly, brushed her teeth and hair, and was still pulling her robe about her as she hurried out.

Connor was leaning moodily against a wall, waiting for her. His chest was still bare, but he had his trousers on and his hair was wet. He must have had a quick sluice under the kitchen tap. He looked magnificent, and Laurel's heart began its irregular pitter-pat before his hand snaked out and grabbed her.

She was pulled into his arms, his hands possessive and familiar now as he pressed her against him. He kissed her slowly, masterfully, demanding the response she was incapable of denying. When she melted against him, he coaxed, 'Stay with me.'

'I can't,' she sighed, leaning her head against his shoulder. 'A freelance is either reliable or unemployed, and I don't care to pay my rent in bed.'

'Damn the rent.'

'That's your point of view. I'm more likely to damn

the landlord, particularly if he doesn't let me go. I'm so late . . .'

Connor tipped her face up to his and asked, 'What was last night about if it wasn't about being together?'

Laurel sighed again, exasperation creeping in. 'There's your work and there's my work, equal priorities, and after that comes us. We can fight about it now or we can talk about it tonight. I don't know about you, but I don't want to fight.'

To her relief he released her, albeit reluctantly. 'Until tonight, then, but I'm not happy. I don't like you rushing off to work.'

'You've been spoilt.' She kissed her fingers, touched them to his lips and got herself into the bedroom before he could grab her again. She reached for the first dress that came out of the wardrobe and dressed with the rapid efficiency of a quick-change artist.

She gathered her accessories together, grabbed her coat, hesitated a moment then went over to the chest of drawers. She opened the top drawer, took out the first of the framed photographs of Lianne, kissed and replaced it. She covered it with a towel, then dug deeper into the corner of the drawer, coming up with a key. Alan's key.

Laurel hesitated for another moment, then hurried into the kitchen. Connor had made tea and had a cup waiting for her. He sipped his while leaning against a kitchen counter, eyed her appreciatively and said, 'The pink dress, now there's a challenge. It's the one I never managed to get off you.'

'Not for the want of trying,' she replied, throwing her coat over a chair and checking she had her bleeper, purse, notebook and other necessary items in her handbag. Then she drank her tea more or less straight down and went over to him.

Connor put his cup aside and took her into his arms. 'You finish at six, right?'

'I should. I'll call if I'm delayed. Where will you be?'

'At home during the day, catching up on the paperwork, but I'll be back here before seven,' he replied, and kissed her.

Laurel leaned against him for a moment, wanting to stay, but habit drew her eyes to her watch. She dropped the key to the flat in his hand and said, 'Just in case I'm late.'

She'd grabbed her handbag and coat and was almost out of the door when he said, 'Take care—and miss me.' Laurel blew him a kiss, stepped over the newspapers on the hall floor, and rushed out of the front door, slamming it behind her.

It seemed so strange, having somebody to leave behind and somebody to come home to. Strange, and wonderful . . . She was several flights down when she heard somebody pounding behind her. She stopped and turned. It was Connor, and he swept her into his arms and kissed her until her senses swam.

'Just wanted to make sure you'd miss me,' he said, and let her go. Laurel touched his cheek lovingly, thinking that, yes, it was very wonderful, and then she fled, not daring to look back in case he came after her again.

Such an easy man to fall for, Connor Dyson, but she seemed to be forever falling for him, over and over again. She was still in a daze when she got to the office, a full fifteen minutes late and saying unkind and utterly untrue things about the traffic. She was normally so dependable, she was actually believed.

Laurel was sent out almost immediately with a photographer to interview an elderly Member of Parliament whose young wife had just given birth to twin boys. It was an easy assignment and it wasn't until after she'd returned to the office and written up the story that she got a chance to look at the day's papers. She skimmed through the headlines of most of them, selecting only one to take down to the canteen with her to read thoroughly over lunch.

She was starving, and as she demolished a cheese salad and crusty rolls she wondered whether Connor had cooked himself a proper breakfast before he'd left, or whether he'd gone straight back to Mayfair. Connor . . . Connor . . . everything she did or thought came back to him, and she kept finding she was smiling idiotically to herself.

It was in this blissfully euphoric state that Laurel read her way more than half-way through the newspaper and found herself staring at the gossip page and a small picture of Letty. She came down from the clouds with a thump as she read the story that went with it:

'The mystery of why fun-loving Lady Letitia Hinds hasn't been out on the town celebrating her newly finalised divorce from Aussie racing driver Carlton Hinds probably lies across the Atlantic. Her long-time boyfriend, Aussie multi-millionaire property tycoon Connor Dyson, has been seen in New York wining and dining his former fiancée, the luscious model-cum-actress Holly Parkes. Could it be that now Lady Letty's free, the marriage-shy Dyson has absconded until yet another hot romance cools down? If so, who's next on his hit list?'

The happiness drained out of Laurel, leaving her feeling cold and empty. She tried to tell herself the story was something fabricated out of nothing, which she knew was what Connor would say. And yet . . . and yet . . . last night he'd asked her all about Alan without ever mentioning his engagement to Holly, or the fact that he'd just met her again.

Wining and dining. What exactly did that mean or, rather, was that all it was? Laurel went colder still as she wondered if Connor had come to her straight from Holly's arms. She felt a flash of pure jealousy, followed by even purer rage.

Chagrin ate into her so that although she remained icy at the centre the rest of her burned, then all feeling drained away, leaving her shattered and exhausted. It was only after this had happened that she began to think again and, in a measure, recover.

The more she thought about how loving Connor had been last night—and this morning!—the less she could believe it had all been lust and deceit. Yet she couldn't quite dismiss the gossip item as total fabrication. In the end, she reserved judgement.

Her love for Connor had grown to the point where it demanded time to be proved one way or the other, and the way things stood, nobody was at risk except herself.

Lianne had never met him, so she couldn't miss him; Aunt Sue and Uncle John knew nothing about him, so they couldn't worry if she was making a fool of herself again.

Somehow, Laurel decided, the situation had to be kept exactly as it was until she developed the trust to back up her love—or discovered she had indeed been the latest on what the gossip columnist described as Connor's 'hit list'.

That evening Laurel vetoed Connor's suggestion of going dancing again, knowing that when she was in his arms she'd believe him if he told her the moon was blue. He only had to touch her and she was wholly his. It was such a lovely way to be that she mourned the loss of her euphoria and wondered wistfully if she had the same effect on him, or whether he was still the hunter and she the nervous prey . . . almost trapped, but still hanging on to enough freedom to keep her interesting.

Was Connor the sort of man who was never satisfied with anything less than a complete kill? She shivered involuntarily and he asked, 'Are you cold?'

'No, just a ghost walking over my grave.'

'You're in the right place for them. This pub is supposed to be a few hundred years old. Parts of it, anyway.' He refilled her wineglass and smiled, and Laurel smiled back.

They were sitting in one of the panelled dining-booths in the ancient pub he had brought her to on their first disastrous date. She'd asked to be brought here again, saying it deserved another chance because it had just the sort of mellow and relaxed atmosphere she appreciated after a hectic day.

The booth gave a cosy sense of intimacy, the steak had been good, and they'd talked about all sorts of things, but nothing of importance. Now, as they sipped their wine and waited for their coffee, Laurel was certain Connor also had something on his mind.

He'd been as charming and attentive as ever, but his usual exuberance was missing. He was quiet, thoughtful and strangely watchful. More than once she'd surprised a frowning, puzzled look in his grey eyes.

The gossip item had been in a popular tabloid, not the sort she'd have expected him to read, but now she was convinced he had. There was no other explanation for his attitude.

He must be trying to puzzle out if she'd also seen it and, if she had, why she hadn't mentioned it. To Laurel's doubting mind, that pointed to guilt. Connor was a blunt man. He'd never pussy-foot around a bone of contention unless he had something to hide.

Let him stew a bit longer, she thought bitterly, and yet her heart ached with loving him and she wished passionately he'd ease the hurt a little by explaining himself without being forced to.

It never crossed her mind that he was waiting for the same thing from her, although for an entirely different reason. It came like a bolt from the blue when, after the coffee had been served, he ran out of patience and said, 'After last night I'd have said we were just about as close as two people could be—but not close enough, it seems, for you to tell me about your daughter. That makes me feel pretty rotten.'

Laurel felt as if she'd had a blow in the solar plexus

and her eyes widened, mirroring her shock. When she could, she breathed, 'How did you find out?'

'Not the way I'd have liked to. I was looking in the chest of drawers this morning for a dry towel so I could shower. I found the photographs. The two shots of you and her were a dead giveaway. When were you going to tell me?'

'I wasn't. At least, not yet.' The reeling world had steadied and Laurel knew that, if she was to expect honesty from him, she had to be honest herself. 'She lives in Hampshire with my aunt and uncle.'

'So that's the big attraction down there.' Connor leaned back in his chair, looking at her sombrely. 'You must have one hell of a cold streak, Laurie, farming out a lovely child like that while you do your own thing in London. I couldn't do it.'

Laurel was so hurt, she said bitterly, 'She's none of your business.'

'I see.' Connor's voice was dangerously quiet and his eyes glittered icily, so that even from the other side of the table she shivered. She felt icy herself as he went on, 'I was forgetting what tidy boxes you keep your life in. We mustn't get them mixed up, must we? That would be too human. I suppose your daughter's in the box marked "Hampshire". Your career must be in the one marked "London". Tell me, lovely lady, which one am I in?'

'The one marked "Bed",' Laurel said savagely, the painful colour of humiliation staining her cheeks, then she got up and walked out on him. She lifted her coat from the rack by the door, threw it on when she was outside, and then the last of her dignity and control left her.

She fled, realised she was heading for the main road where Connor would certainly find her when he'd paid the bill, and turned and ran the other way. The pub was completely rural, with no other sign of habitation. He'd be obliged to take her home, and she couldn't bear that.

Once she was clear of the lights of the pub she had to slow down. The lane was unpaved and deeply rutted, and seemed to be narrowing further as it cut its way through a wood. There was a little moonlight, enough to stop her blundering into the trees, but not enough to see where she was putting her feet.

She stumbled along, her only thought to get away from Connor, and when she heard the roar of his powerful car shatter the silence of the night she stopped and looked fearfully back. She saw the beam of his headlights illuminate the trees opposite the pub, making them stand out against the surrounding darkness with ghostly clarity, then they swung away. He was heading for the road.

Laurel began to breathe a little easier. She stood where she was, listening. Once he was clear, she would go back to the pub and phone for a cab. She was walking back when she heard his car return and saw the headlights dipping and swaying as he drove over the ruts. They seemed to be reaching out for her and she turned and fled once more.

When she was certain he'd passed the pub and was still coming on, she left the lane to find cover among the trees. She'd only gone a few steps when she blundered into a clump of brambles. Her thick coat protected most of her, but she gasped and backed painfully away as thorns tore into her feet.

Connor's headlights caught her and she could have wept with frustration. The car screeched to a halt and then he was striding towards her, big and menacing, with no trace of the man who'd loved her so tenderly. Laurel remembered with a flicker of fear how she'd once thought he wasn't quite tame, and then she was seized by the shoulders and shaken mercilessly.

'What bloody stupid game do you thing you're playing?' he yelled at her. 'Anything could have happened to you out here. I was beginning to think you'd been crazy enough to hitch a lift.'

'I can take care of myself——'

'Don't be any more stupid than you can help,' he cut in furiously, then picked her up, strode to the car, threw her in and slammed the door on her.

Laurel was still straightening herself out when he got in beside her. He leaned across her and she shrank away, but he was only reaching for her seat-belt. 'You should be scared,' he snapped, as he pulled the belt across her and slotted it home. 'I was never closer to throttling anyone in my life.'

She was jolted all over the place as he reversed much too fast along the bumpy lane until he reached the pub and had enough room to turn. When they reached the main road he drove angrily, all acceleration and brakes, but with a savage flair she found exciting.

No matter what he did, he got to her, damn him.

She fought a frantic battle against his magnetism so she could hold on to her own anger, but as time passed she became uneasily conscious that Connor's stony silence spoke more eloquently of his more deeply rooted fury than ever words could have done.

Laurel became conscious of other things, too. The stinging in her feet where the thorns had torn them, Connor's refusal even to glance at her, but mostly—and most depressingly—the fact that, if there was any justice in all this, it was on his side.

She glanced at him and, after a struggle to get the words out, said, 'I'm sorry. I do live my life in boxes and I should have told you about Lianne, but that's all you're right about. You don't understand my reasons at all.'

'I'm listening,' was all the encouragement she got.

Laurel felt rebuffed and she said huffily, 'I can't talk to you if you're still angry.'

Connor glanced at her at last, very coldly. 'I'm going to stay angry for as long as I'm sharing you in some sick sort of way with Curtis.'

'You're not!' Laurel was horrified, and not surprised he was furious if that was what he thought. She just couldn't believe that this was where her well-meaning deception had led her. 'I told you, I despise him.'

'Do you?' Connor asked sceptically. 'You loved him enough to commit yourself to him, you had his child, and he's still running your life.'

'He's not!'

'Yes, he is. For four years he's had you living like a nun, and he's still a barrier between us. He had it all, but if you feel I'm threatening your independence in any way you go straight up the wall. You freeze at the mention of love or commitment. You won't let me help you in any way, when he must be paying for your child——'

'He isn't,' Laurel broke in. 'If he knows about Lianne, it isn't because I've told him. Why do you think I work so damned hard? It's to provide for Lianne, and to prove to myself I can do it without help from anyone. It was something *my* ego needed, for a change. When Alan and I split up I was broke, pregnant and I'd let my career slip. I'd trusted him, you see. Since then I've trusted nobody but myself. I can't change overnight, not for you or anyone else.'

'You've had four years . . .' Connor began.

'It's taken me that long to get straight. Everything was just about coming right when I met you. I wasn't ready.' Laurel paused, then added, 'I'm still not.'

Connor had slackened speed, and she sensed his anger had gone when he said, 'Tell me about it, Laurie. All of it. I need to know if I'm going to get your brains unscrambled.'

'Thanks,' she replied with a wry laugh, 'but I think I'll skip your psychiatric couch. I'll end up in a worse state than I am already. Besides, it's a boring story. It happens all the time.'

'Not to you it doesn't,' he corrected her, 'and therefore not to me.'

Laurel's heart skipped a beat and she gave him a startled glance. She was still trying to figure out the implications of what he'd said when he continued, 'Start with the last time you saw Curtis. I need to be convinced he's totally out of your life.'

'All right. The last time was when he left for the States to take up a job as a TV presenter. The last time I spoke to him was when I phoned to say I was pregnant. He sent me a cheque to have an abortion. I tore it up. End of story.'

'No, it isn't. Why did you have Lianne?' Connor asked.

'Not because she was Alan's, because she was mine, and I've never regretted it.'

'Why did you stay on in the flat?'

'It was cheap and handy,' Laurel told him. 'The agency I was working for didn't pay much, but it was enough to cope, and I was allowed to stay on the newsdesk until Lianne was due. She was born in Hampshire, and when she was three months old my aunt took over and I returned to London to work.' She added with a hint of lingering bitterness against Connor, 'That must have been when my cold streak came into operation, the one that allows me to farm out my child without a second thought.'

'I'm sorry about that,' Connor replied, 'but when I'm hurt, I hurt back. Go on.'

'I'd learned enough with the agency to set up on my own. Whatever you might think, missing so much of Lianne's baby years wasn't easy, but it was the only way I could properly provide for our future. When I move out of Hewitt House we'll have our own home, with a mortgage I can afford. My aunt and uncle are retiring to Spain and, with what I pay them to look after Lianne, I'll be able to hire an au pair to cope while I'm at work. Everything was working out beautifully when I met you.'

Connor said, 'I still don't see why you didn't tell me about Lianne.'

'It's early days for us, Connor, and it was my way of staying as uninvolved as possible while I sorted myself out. This way nobody's life is disrupted but mine. I know I'm over-protective and over-cautious, but that's the effect Alan had on me. I'm trying to do something about it, only you will keep rushing and I need time.'

'How much?' Connor asked laconically. 'Some of us can't live in boxes.'

Laurel bit her lip and looked away. 'I don't suppose I ever really expected it to work, but it seemed worth a shot at the time.' Was this the end, coming so soon after the beginning? If she hadn't been ready to fall in love with Connor, she was even less ready now to fall out of love with him.

She could feel him glancing at her and she was becoming more and more tense as the silence lengthened. Finally he said, 'All right, Laurie, for the time being I'll stay in the box—so long as you tell me it's labelled a bit more than "Bed".'

She turned swiftly towards him, her heart thumping with relief. 'It's a whole lot more than that, Connor. It always was. If I could have walked away from you, I would have. I just couldn't.'

'Fair enough.' He picked her hand out of her lap, kissed it, put it on his thigh and kept his hand over it. Laurel promptly felt loved again, and she leaned across to brush her head against his shoulder in a wordless, tender response.

Connor's hand tightened over hers. 'Promise me something, Laurie. If we fall out, stand and fight. Don't ever run away from me again, not for any reason.'

'I promise,' she replied huskily, 'and I'm sorry.'

'Good. Stay sorry. I don't have a very forgiving nature. Make me mad enough and I won't chase. I won't share you, either. You're going to have to commit yourself to that much.'

'Connor,' Laurel protested, 'I'm in enough trouble coping with you. There isn't going to be anyone else.'

'I don't own much of you, and I want to be sure of what little I do,' he answered uncompromisingly. 'That cuts both ways, of course. I won't be playing around.'

The forgotten gossip item about Holly flashed into Laurel's mind. She opened her mouth to mention it, then closed it again. Like Alan, it was in the past. Connor had given her a definite commitment, the kind she needed most. She would soon know whether she could trust him or not.

'What's wrong with your feet?' Connor asked. 'You keep leaning down to rub them.'

'There were brambles in the woods. My feet got a bit scratched.'

'I hope your toes are all right.'

'Connor, what is it about my toes?' Laurel asked, baffled.

'They were the first things I saw bare about you. They drove me wild. They still do.' He raised her hand to his lips again and kissed it. 'Anything about me get you the same way?'

'Your glasses.'

'My *what*?'

'I know, they're only for the fine print. Just don't waste your time bringing any documents to the flat. You'll never get any work done, I can guarantee that.'

Connor started to laugh and Laurel laughed with him. The euphoria was back with a vengeance.

CHAPTER ELEVEN

LAUREL might have thought she'd been living flat out, but she had to go up a gear to make space for Connor. And yet she was full of energy, as though he'd revitalised her with his love and laughter.

She missed him desperately when he left for New York. She crammed in all the work she could until the weekend, the last one in November, when she whirled down to Hampshire. She swept Lianne into her arms time and again to hug her, then spoilt her with sticky-bun cream teas, trips to the fun-fair and muddy but riotous games of hide-and-seek in the woods.

'What's the matter with you?' Aunt Sue asked. 'You can't seem to be still.'

'I'm excited. I'll soon be shaking the dust of Hewitt House off my feet.' It seemed a treacherous thing to say, since Connor was so much a part of Hewitt House these days, but it was she herself who had told her aunt and uncle he was a womaniser, and sometimes they treated her as though she were no more grown up than Lianne. She didn't want to mar their retirement dream with doubts and fears, especially as she wouldn't be wholly able to reassure them.

Much as she wanted to believe Connor truly loved her, she still had her disquieting moments. He'd asked her to accompany him to New York, which was lovely, and yet he must have known she would refuse. Laurel couldn't quite shake the thought that Holly was there, and he still hadn't mentioned her.

He never mentioned Letty, either. He talked to her of everything else under the sun, but never of the two women she most wanted to know about. It didn't stop her loving him, but it did keep her cautious.

'Have you done anything about a job yet?' Aunt Sue went on.

'I have an interview on the twenty-third of December, which will fit in nicely with the Christmas break,' Laurel replied, still cautiously sticking to her original plan, just in case . . .

But mostly her euphoria held good, and back in London she kept any lurking despondency at bay by working hard. Then Connor was back, sweeping her into his arms and hugging her, pretty much as she had Lianne. He also showered her with designer scarves, handbags, perfume and whatever else had taken his fancy.

'Connor, you mustn't, you know I can't afford things for you,' Laurel protested. 'You'll give me a Cinderella complex.'

'Shut up,' Connor ordered, kissing his way seductively from her ear to her neck. 'They're nothing, and I need to spoil you. Just wait until you let me out of my box.'

'Stop talking about boxes,' she exclaimed vehemently. 'I'm beginning to hate the damn things.'

'Good,' he replied, but he didn't pressure her further. He just kissed her in a way that made coherent thought or speech impossible.

He did grumble, though, as December sped by, that theirs was a catch-as-catch-can relationship. With him working days and she nights, they hardly spent any real length of time together, and Christmas was upon them before they knew it.

They faced another lengthy separation. Connor's parents were due from Australia. They were going to spend a couple of nights in Mayfair, then a few days at Cherisham before flying on to the States to spend the New Year with their eldest daughter, who had married a Californian.

'Can I phone you to wish you a happy Christmas?' Connor asked as they exchanged presents.

'I'll phone you,' she promised, unwrapping a bulky package that had her mystified, and revealing a teddy bear Connor had had custom-made for her. It was wearing a miniature version of his glasses and carrying a miniature briefcase. 'Connor, it's lovely!' she exclaimed, throwing her arms around his neck in genuine delight.

'Open the briefcase,' he ordered, and when she undid the little clasps a string of glowing, perfectly matched pearls fell out.

'Connor, no. They're much too expensive. I told you——'

'You tell me a lot of funny things, and I don't have to listen to all of them,' he told her, taking the pearls and clasping them around her neck. 'There you are, beautiful,' he added, his eyes caressing her. 'The pearls aren't bad, either.'

'Connor . . .' she said lovingly, and kissed him, then watched him unwrap his present. She'd given him black silk pyjamas with his initials picked out in silver thread on the pocket. 'I did that myself,' she told him, 'just to prove that I can be domestic.'

'Whatever gave you the idea I wanted you to be domestic?' he murmured. 'I think you're just trying to make me respectable. You know I never wear pyjamas.'

'So? I never wear pearls, not real ones, anyway. How can I, when everyone will wonder where they came from?'

'Wear them for me, when I'm not wearing my pyjamas,' Connor replied, his grey eyes teasing hers.

He was never serious these days, and Laurel loved him for it, knowing it was his way of keeping pressure off her. It was such a wrench leaving him, and she also had to leave her teddy bear and pearls behind. Otherwise Lianne would think the teddy was for her, and Aunt Sue would want to know about the necklace.

A few hours later she was having her interview. She got the job, but as she drove on to The Pantiles she came out of cloud cuckoo land and found herself face to face with reality. Everything was set now for a neat exit from her London existence when the time came, and she knew she could do no such thing.

Loving, laughing Connor had trampled down her boxes, exposing them for the mockery they had always been . . . as he had known, but she hadn't. Well, she knew now, because she simply couldn't face life without him. He, she and Lianne all had to be together—she could be contented no other way.

She would phone him on Christmas Day and tell him that trust had finally caught up with her love.

The rest would be up to him, and when had Connor ever dragged his feet . . .?

Her decision made, Laurel was conscious of such a tremendous relief that it was only then she realised what a burden she'd been carrying. The ache that was always with her when she was apart from Connor disappeared in a blaze of anticipation. When she and Lianne decorated the tree that afternoon, an excitement that had nothing to do with Christmas spilled out of her.

It kept her awake that night, and it was only when the grey of dawn began to lighten the room that she truly slept, not stirring again until nearly eleven o'clock. It was Christmas Eve. This evening Connor would be bringing his parents down to Cherisham. Tomorrow she would phone, tell her aunt and uncle about him, and then they could all meet up. What a Christmas it would be! The excitement flooded back tenfold.

Laurel went downstairs to discover her uncle had taken Lianne into town to do some last-minute shopping. Aunt Sue didn't grumble about cooking Laurel a late breakfast, in fact she was pleased she'd slept in, but she did complain about her reading the newspaper at the table.

'Just this once?' Laurel pleaded. 'I'll give up my sloppy London ways tomorrow, promise.'

'You should forget all about papers while you're on holiday, give yourself a break,' Aunt Sue told her, but she didn't expect to be listened to and she went back into the kitchen.

Laurel carried on reading as she ate, her eyes

skimming the printed words, her mind on Connor, and when she got to the gossip page she almost choked. Disbelievingly she read:

'The on-off romance of Lady Letitia Hinds and Aussie property tycoon Connor Dyson was on again last night. They were dancing cheek-to-cheek at one of London's most exclusive niteries. Watching benevolently were his parents and hers. A get-together of prospective in-laws before a formal announcement is made?'

There was more, but it was all along the same lines. There was also a picture of Connor and Letty dancing. They were very close.

Laurel tried so hard to be fair. Naturally he would take his parents out and, since he moved in an exclusive circle, naturally he was likely to bump into Letty. But the very last thing he'd said to her was, 'Miss me, Laurie. I'm going to miss you like hell.'

The photographs said differently. There was no mistaking the softness in Connor's eyes as he looked at Letty. Laurel had seen him look too often at herself in just the same way to have any doubts about that. Whatever Letty was to him, she was a darned sight more than just the friend he'd described her as.

Laurel survived Christmas Eve and Christmas Day by playing the part of a woman who had everything to look forward to. She thought privately that she deserved an Oscar, because nobody noticed the difference between her false sparkle and the genuine one she'd arrived home with.

She delayed her promised call to Connor until she was capable of some kind of rational judgement. Half the time she believed he genuinely cared for her, the other half that she'd been duped yet again.

Laurel was incapable of thinking the whole thing through dispassionately, but she could think of only two things that could keep high-living Connor, used to luxury and relaxing at places like Langan's and Stringfellow's, content with Hewitt House and backwater pubs and roadhouses.

One was love, the other that his need to conquer hadn't wholly been satisfied. It could well be that her insistence on keeping her independence, the one thorn between them, was also the tie that bound him to her.

She brooded and doubted until the evening of Boxing Day, when she was driven to the telephone to be put out of her misery one way or the other. Her aunt and uncle were visiting friends and Lianne was fast asleep upstairs.

The telephone at The Pantiles was in the hall, which wasn't heated as well as the rest of the house, but Laurel's fingers trembled with tension rather than chill as she dialled the Cherisham number Connor had given her.

A feminine, friendly Australian voice answered. His mother, she thought, as she asked for him. She heard music and laughter in the background and felt even more forlorn. She couldn't blame Connor for that. It was she who had placed herself firmly outside his circle of family and friends.

All her senses quivered responsively to the sound of his voice on the line, making her despair, so that all she managed to say was, 'Hello.'

'You took your time,' he replied roughly, and Laurel thought it was ironic that, while she had cause, he was the one who was angry. 'Wait a minute, it's noisy in here. I'll switch the call to the library.'

There was a pause, some clicking on the line, then he was speaking again. 'I expected you to call before this. I've been worried, wondering what you were up to.'

'I haven't been up to anything, but there's been some interesting stuff in the paper about you,' Laurel replied as non-committally as she could.

'What stuff?'

She told him. She'd read the piece so many times, she knew it almost by heart.

When she'd finished, Connor said, 'Is that why you didn't phone me, because you believed that rubbish? Laurie, how could you be such a deadhead? I took my parents out for the evening, Letty was out with hers and we picked on the same nightclub. We ended up sharing a table, and that's all there was to it. Honey, I'm not Curtis. You've got to trust me.'

She remembered the photograph and replied quietly, 'I trusted you the last time.'

'What last time?'

'There was a piece about you wining and dining Holly Parkes in New York. It was angled around whether Letty knew what you were up to.'

Connor groaned. 'Laurie, what goes on in that beautiful head of yours? I wasn't up to anything, and if I had been, Letty couldn't have cared less. I told you, there's nothing like that between us. As for

Holly, we happened to find ourselves staying in the same New York hotel and we dined together. It seemed the civilised thing to do, since we'd once been engaged, and I was glad of the chance to pass a rotten evening. I was missing you like mad at the time. I still am.'

'Oh,' Laurel said inadequately, but she was comforted by the fact he sounded exasperated, when surely a guilty man would have been heavily on the defensive?

'Is that all I get—oh?' Connor continued. 'I was hoping to hear you're missing me.'

'I am,' she admitted, 'although it's good to spend some time with Lianne. Are you having a party?'

'I wouldn't call it that, just my parents and a few neighbours. I suppose there's no chance of you coming over? I never feel right unless you're with me.'

That was so much how she felt herself that Laurel's doubts faded and she mentally consigned the gossip items to the dustbin. 'No, but I'm returning to London tomorrow and you'll be there the day after, so it won't be long before we're together. I'm sorry I was so stupid, but if you'd read pieces like that about me, I don't suppose you'd have been too happy, either.'

'I'd have trusted what I know about you, not what some mischief-maker tried to tell me. Promise if you read something like that again you'll talk to me before jumping to all the wrong conclusions.'

'I promise,' Laurel said, meaning it, but the chance of taking Lianne to meet him had gone, and she knew it would take time to build up that much confidence again.

Always at the back of her mind were the 'uncles' that had come and gone in her life during the sham closing years of her parents' marriage. Most of her mother's boyfriends she'd disliked, but there had been one full of fun and laughter she'd grown attached to. She'd felt abandoned when he'd moved on and, in some peculiar way, to blame. For herself, she'd risk anything to be with Connor, but she wouldn't risk Lianne's emotional security.

No, she'd have to wait until she felt wholly sure of him again.

She was hardly given the chance. In the early days of the New Year, Connor said, 'Laurie, I have to go home on Thursday.'

'Home?' Laurel repeated. He had so many of them, she wondered which one he meant.

'Australia.'

She stared at him, dismayed. They'd had such little time together, and it was only two days until Thursday. 'It's a bit sudden, isn't it? Business?'

Connor hesitated fractionally. 'Partly.'

Waiting for him to elaborate, Laurel felt a prickle of unease. It wasn't like Connor to hesitate about anything. Then he went on, 'A friend of mine is getting married. I'll fit that in, too. I'll be gone about ten days, but don't worry if I'm out of touch for a while.'

'I won't,' she replied, knowing that she would. She waited for him to urge her to go with him. She always said no, but that had never stopped him asking. This time he didn't, and she felt desolate, because this time she wouldn't have taken much persuading to say yes.

But she told herself it was her own fault. No man liked to be continually turned down. Next time, she vowed, she'd go with him. And so would Lianne. It was what he'd always wanted, and what she could no longer refuse.

The two days passed like hours, and then she was wrapped in Connor's arms and he was murmuring against her hair, as he always did, 'Miss me, Laurie.'

'Like mad,' she promised, and added something she never had before, 'Try to get back sooner if you can.'

He took her face between his hands and said with a fierceness she didn't understand, 'I wish you weren't a damned reporter.'

Laurel could only suppose he meant the way her job disrupted their lives, and she retorted, 'I wish your work didn't shrink the world to the size of a postage stamp, but I suppose the homecomings make it worth while.'

'You trust me now?' he asked with that same strange fierceness.

'Yes.' Laurel found it was completely true, and was so surprised that she repeated it. 'Yes, so much so that I won't even look at a gossip column while you're away.'

His grey eyes searched hers intently. 'You're mine, then. I mean, you've healed? You're over Curtis and truly mine now?'

Laurel nodded, unable to speak.

Connor shook her gently. 'That's not good enough. Say it.'

'I'm yours. Truly,' she told him huskily.

'That's what I needed to know.' His face lightened into the smile she loved, and he told her, 'Love you when you're mine, Laurie.'

Then he was gone and she faced another endless ten days, but she faced them with the glowing certainty that this separation would be their last.

Laurel filled in the days as she always did when Connor was away, with work and catching up on all the things she'd let slide while he was with her. Two days later she was calling in at the glitzy offices of the magazine where Shirley worked to pick her up for a much overdue lunch.

Shirley grinned and waved her to a seat on the other side of her desk while she finished a phone call, and Laurel looked around, so used to a bustling newsroom, she couldn't imagine what it would be like to work in isolated splendour like this.

When Shirley replaced the phone, she said, 'Hello, stranger. You're looking great.'

'I'm feeling great,' Laurel replied. 'Why so surprised?'

Shirley reached for her handbag, took out her compact and studied her face critically. 'Well, I thought after the thing with Connor Dyson didn't work out . . .'

'It did,' Laurel contradicted, giving her a big smile.

'Oh.' Shirley snapped the compact shut. 'Well, that's great. Let's go.'

'Hang on a minute, what made you think it didn't?' Laurel asked, her smile fading into a puzzled frown.

'Not a thing. You know me, always getting hold of

the wrong end of the stick.'

'Yes, I do know you,' Laurel replied slowly, 'well enough to know you don't say things like that off the top of your head. You're often scatty, but you're not malicious. What made you say it?'

'Oh, damn,' Shirley muttered, 'I wish I'd kept my big mouth shut. Are you in deep with him?'

'About as deep as I can get.' Laurel tried to speak lightly, but anxiety was twisting within her, and fear. 'What do you know that I don't?'

'Hell, it's probably nothing. I'm surprised you haven't seen it, anyway.' She flicked through a pile of magazines and newspapers, and pulled one out. 'It's yesterday's. I have to go through them all to see if there's anything I can follow up. Many a fine feature has been born in a gossip snippet, those that stand up. Many of them don't, but you know that.'

Laurel was paging through the paper with unsteady fingers, and then she found it. There was no picture this time, but the item didn't really need one. It brought her world crashing down, and it was only one paragraph. The columnist must know he was on to something, because he just wasn't letting up, Laurel thought, as she read:

'In a devious attempt to escape notice, Aussie property tycoon Connor Dyson and Lady Letitia Hinds jetted separately to Paris before boarding the same plane to Australia. Who do the love-birds think they are fooling?'

Every word struck Laurel like a physical blow, but the one that struck hardest was 'devious'. Connor, her lovely Connor, had completely duped her. If he had nothing to hide about Letty, there was no reason for the separate flights to Paris, no reason why he shouldn't have told her they were travelling together.

In fact, he'd have made sure she'd known just to keep everything above board, and he would certainly have asked her to accompany him. Instead, he'd only insisted she tell him she was truly his. A question from the heart, she'd thought, but it had only been from the ego. He'd needed to know he had her where he wanted her at last.

'Laurel, are you all right?' Shirley asked anxiously.

'No, but I will be,' Laurel replied, carefully folding the newspaper and returning it to the pile. 'I wasn't a complete fool this time. I was very careful not to wrap my whole life around him. It was great while it lasted, but now that he's gone there'll scarcely be a ripple. I can live with that.'

She stood up and pinned a big false smile on her face. 'Now, what about that lunch? I'm starving.' But she didn't quite meet Shirley's eyes, and Shirley's didn't quite meet hers. They both knew she couldn't talk about Connor any other way without cracking up completely.

CHAPTER TWELVE

LAUREL had so much organised already that it was surprisingly easy to cut and run. She phoned the county paper she was due to join at the beginning of March, and they said, fine, they would be happy to have her start a month earlier.

Then she phoned Aunt Sue to say Hewitt House was so depressing, now that virtually all the flats were empty, that she was moving in with Shirley for a couple of weeks, then she would be home for good.

'What about your things?' Aunt Sue asked, ever practical.

'There's not a lot I want to bring with me—just my books, clothes and some electrical equipment. I've hired a firm specialising in small removals and you can expect the stuff on Monday. I've arranged to start my new job at the beginning of February, so there are no problems there. I just have to finish up the commitments I've already made. Is that all right?'

'It sounds a marvellous idea. It will give Lianne time to get so used to you around that she won't miss us so much. What about an au pair?' Aunt Sue asked.

'I'll arrange to interview some while I'm at Shirley's. If I find someone suitable, I'll bring her down with me. Will that be all right with you?'

'It will be useful to have someone take Lianne off my hands while I do my own packing,' Aunt Sue confessed, 'and I'll be easier in my own mind to know you're out of that horrid Hewitt House.'

Horrid, Laurel thought, as she replaced the phone a little later and looked around the flat. Horrid wasn't a word she would have used. For a little while it had been paradise . . .

There were a lot of Connor's possessions scattered in every room and, because they were his, she'd never minded the clutter, nor had she minded the way her own washing and ironing had piled up. She must really have loved him, she thought vaguely. She was so numb, nothing was really getting through to her.

It was the numbness that was her greatest ally. She felt as though she were playing the part of Laurel Curtis, and that all this wasn't really happening to her at all. It had been so different when she'd been clearing Alan out of her life. She'd been angry then. Now there was only this—this nothing.

She packed Connor's things first, along with the pearls he'd given her, and mailed them to the Mayfair house. Then she sent a separate business letter to Dyson Enterprises (UK) Ltd, formally vacating the flat and requesting the cheque due to be sent to her solicitor.

After that there were only meter readings to be sent to the gas and electric companies, asking for the bills to be sent to The Pantiles, and that was it. She was on her way to Shirley's with just a suitcase of necessary clothes.

It was a good, clean break, just as she'd always planned, and this time her heart wasn't broken. It couldn't be, because she still wasn't feeling anything at all.

Laurel didn't see much of Shirley because they worked such different hours, but Shirley saw enough of her to say uneasily, 'I wish you'd shout, scream, cry, break something! You're like a zombie. It's not natural. I think you're in shock.'

'Phooey,' Laurel mocked, smiling. 'I saw the end of this . . . thing . . . with Connor before I saw the beginning. Bless your romantic heart, Shirley, but what you're seeing is not a zombie but a realist. I'm fine, honest.'

For a while she really believed it. She almost had Shirley believing it.

It wasn't until she moved down to The Pantiles—finally achieving her four-year dream—that the numbness began to wear off and the hurt began.

With it came thoughts that tortured her, and sensations that were even worse. She would imagine Connor touching her, and the feeling was so real that her flesh would quiver. She would see him smiling at her, and smile back at nothing. She would hear his laughter and turn her head towards it, to find it was only an echo in her agonised mind.

Worst of all, she would awake some mornings, so certain he was beside her, it was the most devastating shock to find just an empty space. It happened time and again, until she felt she was going mad.

And threaded through it all were her thoughts, twisting the knot of pain within her ever tighter. She'd never told him where The Pantiles was, but he could find her if he wanted to. There were always ways. As a reporter, she could think of several, and

Connor had unlimited means at his disposal. He wouldn't even have to exert himself, simply hire somebody.

He never tried, and she forced herself to accept that her disappearance must have been nothing more to him than an unexpected favour. Connor obviously didn't want an ex-mistress cluttering up his life unless, like the others, she was willing to be available when it suited him. She wasn't, so it was bye-bye Laurie.

Laurie . . . She cringed as the longing to hear him say her name once more swept over her. She remembered the things she loved most about him . . . the glasses for the small print . . . the scars on his lip and eyebrow which he'd told her were old rugby injuries . . . the lines on either side of his mouth he'd sworn had never been dimples.

Such silly things to go all gooey over, but they had made him seem vulnerable, and there wasn't much about Connor that was.

It seemed to Laurel, as day followed day, that the hurt wasn't healing but becoming more acute. She felt as though slowly, bit by bit, she was crumbling into the glaring great hole he had left in her life. What made it all the worse was having to behave as though none of this was happening to her. She was the woman who had achieved her dream, and she had to behave as though she had. It was the stinging backlash of being too protective, too cautious and too clever for her own good.

How she managed it she didn't know, but nobody suspected her misery. She had two things to help her,

her genuine joy at being with Lianne, and her aunt's preoccupation with endless lists as she prepared for the retirement to Spain.

Then there were more practical things. The Dutch au pair Laurel had chosen because she was cheerful and homely had to be drawn into the family circle and taught the routine Lianne was used to, and January ground into February so that Laurel had to begin her first staff job in years.

It all helped, or Laurel thought it did, until she found herself always turning to the gossip pages of the newspapers first, hungry for news of Connor, even if it only deepened the pain. She never found any items there, but he was mentioned in the business columns once. His company had branched into Europe, as he had said it would.

Laurel thought of the lunch in Paris that she'd missed, and wondered who Connor was asking now. Somehow she didn't think it was Letty. There had been no mention of her in the papers at all. Perhaps Letty had discovered, in some painful way, she was only sharing Connor's favours. It was strange, Laurel mused, that her own obsession with secrecy must have helped to keep that affair alive.

Her new job went some way towards helping February pass more quickly than the catalytic January, and then there was the upheaval of her aunt and uncle moving to Spain. Lianne was more excited than tearful, buoyed up by Laurel's promise that they would go to the villa in the summer for a lovely holiday.

The Pantiles settled into its new routine. For some

time Laurel had been fighting the urge to get in touch with Connor, if only to hear his voice once more. More than once she'd actually dialled his number, only to panic and throw down the receiver. The weeks without him had weakened, not strengthened her.

Just a telephone call, she told herself. A little chat between friends to show there were no grudges. She had to do something, she just couldn't go on like this, nursing a desperate need that wouldn't go away. Yet every time she made that call she couldn't go through with it. Connor didn't want her. If he was sharing her kind of agony, he'd have done something about it. He was that sort of man.

By the end of the first week in March, Laurel's physical and emotional exhaustion began to tell. On Saturday morning she just couldn't drag herself out of bed until nearly eleven. It was a lovely day and Greta, the au pair, had taken Lianne and Shadow for a walk.

Laurel made herself a cup of tea, and sat down to drink it. The newspaper was on the table and she half-heartedly turned it towards her so she could see the headlines. She never did read them, because there on the front page was a picture of Letty laughing up at a handsome young man. She recognised him instantly. It was racing driver Carlton Hinds.

'It's happiness second time around for racing ace Carlton Hinds and Lady Letitia, daughter of the Earl of Darrow. Flying into London last night, they revealed that they secretly remarried in Australia in January, less than a month after their divorce was finalised. They have been honeymooning on Carlton's Queensland sheep station, where the second marriage took place. Best man, also second time around, was property tycoon Connor Dyson, once tipped as Lady Letitia's husband No. Two. Asked about that, Carlton said, "Connor and me have been good mates for years. He was only keeping an eye on her for me, and doing his best to talk her into seeing me again, so I could convince her what a big mistake the divorce had been." Why all the secrecy? Lady Letitia explained, "There was so much publicity surrounding our first marriage, we never really had time to settle down to married life. We were determined that wouldn't happen again."'

The paper dropped from Laurel's nerveless fingers and she stared blankly at the kitchen wall. What had she done? Good heavens, what had she done?

Connor hadn't failed her, she'd failed him. He must have returned to the flat to find—nothing. Not even a note. Laurel closed her eyes and flinched, imagining his bewilderment, his pain and—being Connor—his anger. How betrayed he must have felt. No wonder he hadn't tried to find her.

She'd promised him that if she was ever in doubt again she'd talk to him before jumping to all the wrong conclusions. The day he'd left she'd assured him she trusted him and she was truly his. And then she'd let him come home to a boarded-up flat.

Laurel began to shiver violently, imagining what she'd put him through. In a daze she went upstairs to her bedroom, pulled open her wardrobe and took from the top shelf the one thing he'd given her that she hadn't been able to part with, the teddy bear with glasses and briefcase.

She sat down on her bed, hugging it, hearing him say as clearly as if he were with her, 'I don't have a very forgiving nature. Make me mad enough and I won't chase.'

Laurel turned her head and looked at her reflection in the dressing-table mirror. She was thinner, there were mauve smudges under her eyes, and whatever sparkle she'd had was gone. She had to simulate it now with make-up and, at the weekends, she simply didn't bother.

If Connor met her now he wouldn't look at her twice—or would he? It was hard to believe the magnetism between them depended entirely on looks, because she'd met handsome men without her interest being stirred, and he must have met lovelier women than her. Perhaps it was still there. Perhaps just looking at each other again was the only spark necessary to ignite it.

In any case, she had to talk to him again, apologise, try to explain. She owed him that much. Sending him a yellow rose this time wouldn't be enough. She doubted whether her head on a platter would be.

Laurel sighed, put down the teddy bear and reached for the phone extension beside her bed. It was Saturday. If Connor was in England, he'd be at Cherisham. She pressed the numbers so nervously, she made a mistake and had to start again.

'Dyson.' His voice was on the line was quickly, so curt, she wasn't ready for it. Her throat dried up and she couldn't say a word. He repeated irritably, 'Dyson.'

Laurel licked her lips. 'It's me,' she replied softly, foolishly. There was no answer and she added wretchedly, 'Laurel.' Had he forgotten her voice so soon?

No, he hadn't. He said harshly, 'If you've got something to say to me at last, Laurel, come and say it to my face.'

The dialling tone buzzed in her ear. Connor had hung up on her, and he'd called her Laurel. She knew then that there would be no kisses, only castigation, but she had to go, she had to try . . . and right away, before she lost her courage.

She left a note for Greta saying she'd had to pop out but she wouldn't be long, so certain was she that Connor only wanted her at Cherisham to have the satisfaction of throwing her out. She brushed her hair, otherwise she went exactly as she was, in jeans and a loose sweater and without make-up.

She didn't look much like Connor's golden girl. Well, he probably had another one by now. Somebody uncomplicated, who didn't break her promises. Pain twisted within her, but it was followed by reason. Connor didn't have a sadistic streak. He wouldn't bring her to Cherisham if he had another woman there. He couldn't want to hurt her that much . . .

Laurel had never been to the manor before, but it was well signposted and she had no trouble finding it. She had no trouble falling in love with it, either. The house was long, low and rambling with a quaint gabled-attic roof. It was mellow and rustic rather than grand, a home rather than a show-piece.

But Laurel's impressions were jangled and chaotic, reflecting her emotions. She parked and sat there for a few seconds, trying to rehearse what she would say. Nothing came. Her mind was a blank. It was her nerves and senses that were working overtime.

She felt an overwhelming urge to flee, to avoid what could only be a traumatic confrontation, but some need to atone, some scrap of hope, got her out of the car and impelled her towards the front door. She grasped the ancient iron bell-pull and was surprised when it worked.

Laurel was even more surprised when Connor opened the door. She was expecting a housekeeper or a manservant, some moments of grace in which to pull herself together. But she was looking straight into Connor's steel-grey eyes and they were cold and impersonal.

She knew then that she should never have come, because her eyes were searching his face with a hunger that had only increased with the weeks of separation. 'Hello, Connor,' she said awkwardly.

'Hello, Laurel.' His voice was as cold and impersonal as his eyes, and he stood back for her to enter.

She found herself in a small panelled hall, and as he closed the door behind her she was conscious of his closeness. She wished she could walk into his arms and cling to him, hoping that the magic would still be there and words would be unnecessary. She couldn't. He'd called her Laurel again in that hateful way, and that made him as remote and untouchable as a stranger.

She quivered as he brushed past her to lead the way along a passage full of unexpected alcoves and twists and turns, which showed how much the interior of the house had been altered over the generations. Laurel, however, was conscious only of the tall figure she followed, and his hostility.

Connor opened a door and stood waiting for her to enter. She quivered again as she walked past him into a long, narrow room with bookcases on either side of a deeply recessed stone fireplace, in which huge logs crackled and blazed. There were well-worn leather armchairs and a chesterfield. The opposite wall was a series of embrasures where leaded windows thrust out into a cobbled stableyard. Outside, big tubs spilled out ivy, aubrietia and tulips.

Laurel heard the click as Connor closed the door and felt the flutter of nerves in her stomach. There was no escape now. She was trapped with Connor's anger and her own hopeless feeling of inadequacy.

Connor didn't ask her to sit down and he didn't sit down himself, either. He strode past her and leaned against the wall next to one of the windows. He was wearing jeans, and Laurel longed to bury her face in the rough wool of his cream sweater, but then he folded his arms. Body language, she thought. He's shutting himself in, me out.

She stood there awkwardly in the middle of the room, feeling like an errant schoolgirl in front of the headmaster, but she couldn't smile at the absurdity of it. This was all too serious and real—and this, unless she could get through to him, would be where she finally lost Connor forever.

'You look bloody terrible,' he said, and Laurel flinched as though he'd struck her.

'I've been missing you,' she whispered, then made

another effort to pull herself together. She had to do better than this. 'I'm sorry, Connor, so terribly sorry.'

'And that's it?' he asked, and she could hear the anger beginning to burn through his icy control. 'Well, it isn't enough. Yesterday it would have been, but today it isn't. You haven't come back because of anything I've ever said or done. You've come back because of this.'

He snatched up a newspaper from the window-seat and flung it at her. It struck her shoulder and fell in a scatter of pages at her feet. 'You had to read in the paper that you could trust me,' he went on savagely. 'You couldn't trust me by yourself. Do you know what it was like, Laurel, to come back to nothing, nothing at all—except broken promises? Well, I tell you, I'm never going through that again.'

'Why didn't you explain about Letty?' she cried. 'Why didn't you trust me?'

'The way you trusted me?' he mocked. 'As a matter of fact I did, but I couldn't persuade Letty to. She doesn't trust any reporter. It was stuff she read about Carl that broke up her marriage in the first place. She made me promise not to tell you. I didn't like it, but I thought we'd passed the point where anything could separate us. I thought we were too close, too certain. I thought a lot of bloody stupid things.'

'Connor, those things weren't stupid, they were real. You have to understand the way I am——'

'I've been understanding you for weeks,' he broke in bitterly. 'I've made concessions and allowances I'd never have made for anybody else. I didn't pressure you. I gave you all the time you asked for, and where did it get me? Right back where I started. When I needed you to believe in me, you still couldn't separate me from Curtis.'

Despair washed over Laurel, and she said desperately, 'That's not true, Connor. I love you. I always have.'

'It's not any kind of love I understand.' He turned his back on her and stared out of the window.

She was dismissed, but she couldn't move. Her love and longing trapped her here. 'Don't,' she begged, 'please don't turn your back on me. I've missed you so much . . . I can't tell you how many times I've nearly phoned you.'

'Nearly might be good enough for you, but it isn't for me.'

'Connor, *please*! Don't be like this. I feel as if I'm dying.'

He swung round and faced her, his eyes like flint. 'Don't expect me to bleed for you. I've been through all that myself.' He nodded across the room. 'There's the door. Do what you always do when things don't work out the way you think they should—run away.'

'Run?' Laurel exclaimed. 'I can't even walk. I have to stay. I can't live without you. I just can't!'

Connor's eyes blazed and she flinched as he strode towards her, expecting to be seized and thrown out bodily. She was grabbed, and thoroughly shaken, but then she was clasped in his strong arms and nearly crushed to death.

'Laurie, the hell I've been through to hear you say that,' he told her roughly. 'I was beginning to think you never would.'

She buried her face in his thick sweater and whispered brokenly, 'I'm so sorry, but why didn't you come looking for me? Why——?'

'I needed you to come to me. It's the only way I could be sure you'd never run away again.' Connor kissed her hair in that familiar way that made her ache with love for him. 'I need to be certain of you, just as you need to be certain of me. It's something that never seems to have crossed your mind.'

He tried to lift her face to his, but Laurel resisted. 'No, don't look at me. I look terrible, you said so.'

He forced her face up anyway and smiled down at her, his grey eyes tender. 'Love you when you look terrible, Laurie,' he said softly.

Her eyes filled with tears. He kissed them away and then he kissed her lips. Laurel felt all the misery and pain drain out of her and she said tremulously, 'I do love you so, Connor. Tell me we're all right now. Tell me everything's all right.'

He put her away from him, took her hand and led her out of the room. 'We'll go and get Lianne, then we'll be right.'

Laurel followed him dazedly, telling him, 'There's an au pair as well.'

'We'll take the station-wagon.'

'And a dog.'

Connor stopped and pulled her into his arms again. 'I don't care if there's a camel. Whatever it takes to get you under my roof.'

Pure happiness shot through Laurel, and she said with a wavering smile, 'Stop being so nice. You'll make me cry again.'

'I'll make you howl if I get any more nonsense from

you,' he threatened, 'and that includes worrying about what the papers will say about us. We'll get married just as soon as I can fix it, but in the meantime tell me you don't give a damn about anything like that.'

'I don't give a damn—bully,' she whispered.

'I'll only bully you when it's strictly necessary, which will probably be six days out of seven. Scared?'

'Terrified,' Laurel told him, winding her arms around his neck and kissing him. 'Thanks for telling me we're getting married. I wasn't sure.'

'I've always been sure, it's just taken you a heck of a long while to catch up with me.' Connor unwound her arms from his neck, kissed her hands and held them. 'Can we go and get Lianne now? I can't wait to spoil you both to death.'

Laurel's eyes misted. 'You don't have to spoil us. You just have to love us.'

'That's no problem. It never was.'

'Oh.' Laurel hid her face in his shoulder and cried in earnest.

'Stop that,' Connor ordered. 'I'm an easygoing fellow, but the one thing you're not allowed to do is cry.' Still her tears flowed, faster than he could mop them up or kiss them away. Desperately he said, 'Love you when you cry, Laurie.'

It took a little while, but it did the trick. Laurel stopped crying and smiled.

H A R L E Q U I N
Romance®

Coming Next Month

Available in June wherever paperback books are sold, or through Harlequin Reader Service:

In the U.S.
901 Fuhrmann Blvd.
P.O. Box 1397
Buffalo, N.Y. 14240-1397

In Canada
P.O. Box 603
Fort Erie, Ontario
L2A 5X3

Have You Ever Wondered If You Could Write A Harlequin Novel?

Here's great news—Harlequin is offering a series of cassette tapes to help you do just that. Written by Harlequin editors, these tapes give practical advice on how to make your characters—and your story—come alive. There's a tape for each contemporary romance series Harlequin publishes.

Mail order only

All sales final

Indulge a Little
Give a Lot

A LITTLE SELF-INDULGENCE CAN DO
A WORLD OF GOOD!

Last fall readers indulged themselves with fine romance and free gifts during the Harlequin®/Silhouette® "Indulge A Little—Give A Lot" promotion. For every specially marked book purchased, 5¢ was donated by Harlequin/Silhouette to Big Brothers/Big Sisters Programs and Services in the United States and Canada. We are pleased to announce that your participation in this unique promotion resulted in a total contribution of *$100,000*.

*

Watch for details on Harlequin® and Silhouette®'s
next exciting promotion in September.